MORTAL CHAOS

'I loved it. I read it cover to cover just in this weekend which I have never done before! I could not put it down as I always needed to know what happened next.' OLIVER

'An amazing story that hooked me from the first line. Breathtaking, exciting and terrifying. I loved it.' MAIRÉAD

'Seeing how a beat of a butterfly's wing can set in motion a chain of events that ends in catastrophe made me look more closely at the small things that happen in life. It was an intriguing concept in a fascinating story.' KIERAN

'*Mortal Chaos* was a gripping, rapid read that had me on tenterhooks. I would definitely recommend this book to friends.' DANIEL

'I never usually notice the little things that happen around me but this book shows just how important tiny happenings are . . . that a butterfly can change so much in the world. Matt made the story so exciting and thrilling.' EWAN

'It was gripping from the first page. Everything that happened was breathtaking and made you not want to put the book down.' DAISY

Matt Dickinson

MORTAL CHAOS

OXFORD
UNIVERSITY PRESS

OXFORD
UNIVERSITY PRESS

Great Clarendon Street, Oxford OX2 6DP

Oxford University Press is a department of the University of Oxford.
It furthers the University's objective of excellence in research, scholarship,
and education by publishing worldwide in

Oxford New York

Auckland Cape Town Dar es Salaam Hong Kong Karachi
Kuala Lumpur Madrid Melbourne Mexico City Nairobi
New Delhi Shanghai Taipei Toronto

With offices in

Argentina Austria Brazil Chile Czech Republic France Greece
Guatemala Hungary Italy Japan Poland Portugal Singapore
South Korea Switzerland Thailand Turkey Ukraine Vietnam

First published 2012

British Library Cataloguing in Publication Data
Data available

ISBN: 978-0-19-275713-5

1 3 5 7 9 10 8 6 4 2

Printed in Great Britain
Paper used in the production of this book is a natural,
recyclable product made from wood grown in sustainable forests.
The manufacturing process conforms to the environmental
regulations of the country of origin.

For my son,
Ali

1

07.37 GMT, SAUNCY WOOD, WILTSHIRE, UK

The butterfly was a Purple Hairstreak, a newborn female, still sticky from her chrysalis as she climbed the oak sapling and tested the morning air. It was a chill June start to the day, with the promise of summer heat to come, the silverweed and red campion around her spun with brilliant gossamer, tendrils of dawn mist still woven through the grass.

Proboscis unfurled, she fed for a while, then—sated on honeydew—opened her wings for the first time.

She was a dark, beautiful creature, almost perfectly black in this first moment of exposure, the velvet texture of her sharply tipped wings seeming to absorb the light. She shivered a little, her antennae vibrating as each hindwing fluttered in turn, drying out the dampness of her long incarceration.

Her scales began to change, the black yielding quite suddenly to create two shadowy pools of purple pigment on each forewing. They were dazzlingly iridescent, shaped like drop pearls, arrayed in perfect symmetry from the thorax.

The first rays of sunlight filtered through a nearby coppice of ash. Caught up in the wonder of what she had become, the butterfly launched herself from the sapling and flew.

2

MOOREND GALLOP, WILTSHIRE, UK

Keiron Wallace shortened the reins on Mazarine Town, raising himself expertly in the saddle as she moved smoothly into the gallop, the rhythmic pounding of her hooves drumming crisply on the turf, her breath coming in eager bursts. The jockey encouraged the thoroughbred with a few murmured words, enjoying the cold rush of morning air on his cheeks and the intoxicating sensation of power as the white furlong markers of the training run flashed by.

Moments later, Beaumont Boy was pulling even at his side, Keiron's stablemate Gary Price in the saddle. 'I thought this was just a warm up,' he called to Keiron as he tried to keep pace, 'we don't want to burn them out for the race.'

'Do 'em good to have a burst,' Keiron told him, 'it'll help 'em settle. Plus a fiver says I beat you to the woods.'

Gary couldn't resist the challenge, and put some pressure on Beaumont Boy with his knees, hoping that stable owner Mike Sampson wasn't spying on them with his binoculars. Both horses were racing at Newbury later that day and the owner would be furious if he thought his jockeys had pushed their mounts too hard on the training session.

'Get a move on,' Gary goaded him as he edged forward, 'what's wrong with you?'

The two jockeys pushed harder into the gallop, caught up now in the spirit of the duel.

Suddenly they were out of the windswept heath and entering the forested section of the ride, the trees flashing past as the two horses lengthened their strides and picked up their speed yet further.

3

SAUNCY WOOD, WILTSHIRE, UK

The rabbit was a doe, just twenty days old and barely weaned. The strongest of her litter, she was the first to brave the journey through the dark walls of the warren on her way to the verdant wonders of the outside world. Emerging warily from the hole, she blinked as her eyes adjusted to the morning light. Then her pink nose twitched with excitement as she saw others of her kind.

She took a hop towards them, then, losing her nerve, scuttled back into the hole. But the aroma of fresh vegetation was too enticing and she was soon back out to nibble at some fresh shoots of grass.

Then, in an instant, the mood around her changed. The rabbits stopped grazing as a thunderous beating noise began to fill the morning air. The very ground was vibrating as the drumming, pulsating beats resonated through the young doe's body. Thump. A buck beat an alarm with his hind legs as rabbits scattered in all directions.

Her heart jumping, the young rabbit scuttled first one way, then the other as the adults around her rushed for cover.

She could have controlled herself, in fact she was at the very moment of running into the nearest hole, when a dark fluttering creature descended from the sky and began to fly around her. The rabbit took a small hop, hoping to lose the tormentor; but the butterfly followed her, skipping and dancing on the morning air.

The rabbit took a few fast jumps into longer grass but the

butterfly followed again, fluttering unpredictably around her. Then the black butterfly brushed against the rabbit's back and that was when the young doe lost all sense of direction and bolted.

4

MOOREND GALLOP, WILTSHIRE, UK

Mazarine Town and Beaumont Boy were side by side on the fastest section of the gallop when the rabbit shot out of the woods beside them. It happened so fast that Keiron never really had a chance to register what was happening. All he saw was a flash of fur as the tiny creature ran at full tilt beneath the horses' hooves. Mazarine Town lost her footing for a startled second, bringing her head down, sending Keiron flying out of the saddle as she went into the fall.

Keiron put himself into a roll, cradling his head and neck in his hands and praying that Mazarine Town wouldn't land on top of him as she hit the ground. By good fortune the horse did miss him, her aluminium-clad hooves narrowly avoiding his head as she skidded sideways alongside him and came—wide-eyed and frothing—to a halt. Keiron was up on his feet in an instant, reaching for Mazarine Town's reins and calming her with a few words: 'Whoa, girl, take it easy, take it easy now.'

Gary had brought Beaumont Boy to a stop. Now he trotted back and dismounted next to Keiron as Mazarine Town climbed slightly shakily back to her feet.

'What the hell was that about?'

'I think it was a rabbit startled her.'

'Are you OK?'

Keiron rubbed his chest, feeling his ribs already sore from the fall. He'd had a lot worse.

'Yeah, got away with it.'

'And the rabbit?' Gary looked around but could see no sign.

'Stuff the bunny, mate. What about the horse? The Guv'nor'll lose it big time if she's lame.'

'Walk her round.'

Keiron let Mazarine Town regain some of her composure then led her by the nose, starting her at a walk and then breaking her into a gentle canter as he ran beside her.

5

SAUNCY WOOD, WILTSHIRE, UK

The rabbit was still running for her life, moving deeper into the woods on the far side of the gallop, instinctively trying to put distance between herself and those thundering, flashing hooves that had so nearly crushed the life out of her.

An acute stress reaction was setting in, the shock of the narrow escape quickly overwhelming the small animal. She began to shake as her heart went into tachycardia.

The rabbit stopped, crawled beneath some low-lying vegetation for cover and lay there panting as the sound of the creatures and their riders in the chase slowly faded.

There was pain in her flank. She licked tentatively at the fur and tasted blood. Branches above her suddenly moved as a gust of wind ran through the trees. The rustling unnerved her and she broke cover again, hopping erratically on a random path through the dark forest, wanting more than anything to find the welcoming burrows where she belonged.

Quickly she became hopelessly lost, moving continually in the wrong direction. Her disorientation was not surprising; the newborn creature had no experience of the outside world to draw upon. All she had ever known was the earthy embrace of the tunnels where she had been born. The world to her was a big, bright, bewildering mystery and her first outing had been a hostile encounter which had almost ended in a violent death.

No wonder the poor creature was utterly freaked out.

6

MOOREND GALLOP, WILTSHIRE, UK

'I don't like the look of that foreleg.' Gary pointed to Mazarine Town's left leg. 'She's favouring the right.'

Keiron ran her again, watching carefully for any sign of a limp. Once or twice he thought he might have seen what Gary was talking about, but then the horse would put in a few smoother strides and she looked well.

'I'm not so sure.'

'Better get her checked out by the vet when we get back to the yard.'

Keiron mounted the horse, running his hand along her neck to soothe her.

'Let's not bother. What they don't know won't hurt 'em, right?'

'You've got to tell the boss about the fall.'

Keiron knew Gary was right. Mazarine Town was a hell of a valuable horse and you never could tell with injuries. If she developed a problem later in the day, and it emerged that he had failed to tell the owner about the fall, Keiron would get docked a week's wages at the very least. Besides, he was supposed to be riding her in the twelve thirty race at Newbury.

'OK, we'll tell the boss. But back me up about the rabbit, right?'

'Yeah, I saw it clear as day.'

The two jockeys rode back to the yard and told owner Mike Sampson about the fall. Sampson, distinctly unimpressed with the news, got straight on his mobile to the local vet who specialized in racehorse injuries.

'Morning, Howard,' the owner growled. 'Any chance you could come over to the yard?'

'What's the problem?'

'One of my damn fool jockeys has given Mazarine Town a tumble and she's supposed to run at Newbury later today. I need her checked out asap.'

'On my way,' the vet told him. 'I'll be with you in ten minutes.'

7

EVEREST SUMMIT RIDGE, NEPAL

At that precise moment, six time-zones away, on the lethal slopes of Mount Everest's North Face, an eighteen-year-old Japanese girl by the name of Kuni Hayashi was fighting her way through deep snow towards the highest point on Earth.

This talented young climber knew the risks she was facing; she understood all too clearly that avalanche, a collapsing serac above her, or a sudden savage storm could snatch her life away.

The concept that something from *outside* her direct environment might screw things up for her was not something she had thought much about. Here, climbing solo in the rarified air of extreme altitude, she felt utterly isolated. Somehow separate from the teeming world beyond.

But that was an illusion; no world, however remote, is immune to the insidious effects of chaos theory and before the day was out, the dynamics of Kuni's climb would be twisted most cruelly out of shape by the long reach of the butterfly effect.

Right now it was 1.45p.m. local time and Kuni was standing at the foot of the notorious Second Step, a sheer wall of crumbling rock which was slick with black ice. If she could make it up the lethal cliff then the summit might be hers—and with it the honour, aged eighteen, of becoming the youngest woman ever to solo Mount Everest.

This was the most dangerous climbing challenge on the

North Face of Everest and she paused to draw super chilled air into her lungs. Even for a star climber like Kuni, this would be a severe test.

If she failed, she would fall seven thousand feet down the sheer North Face, her body hurtling down to destruction in the climbers' graveyard on the glacier below.

8

SILSBURY VILLAGE, WILTSHIRE, UK

'How did she fall?' the vet asked Keiron.

'Got startled by a rabbit.'

'How fast was she running?'

'Well, it wasn't much more than a canter,' the forelorn-looking jockey lied, 'it was just a warm up.'

'OK. Walk her round.'

The jockey led the horse on a right-hand circuit of the yard, then a left as the vet watched with his expert eye.

'There *could* be a tendon strain here. Maybe even a small tear,' Howard said. 'But if there is, it doesn't seem to be bothering her overmuch. We could give her an MRI scan,' the vet told them, 'if you really wanted to be a hundred per cent sure.'

The owner Mike Sampson considered the idea, but also bore in mind the time pressure of getting the horse over to Howard's clinic. That would almost certainly mean missing the race.

'What's your gut feeling?'

Howard took an appraising look at the horse, noting she didn't seem to be in any discomfort.

'I think she's sound.'

'Would you come up to Newbury with us? Check her out just before the race?'

The vet flicked through his personal organizer, finding that his only other booking was a routine inspection on a pregnant mare at another stables—an easy enough appointment to move. Besides, a day at the races was one of the perks of the job and if he knew Mike Sampson the booze would be flowing whether he had a winner or not. 'You're on,' he told the owner, 'but I'll have to pop home and check Will's off to school.'

'All right, lads,' the owner told Keiron and Gary, 'get the horses loaded in the box, we'll take a risk on Maz, she doesn't look so bad. And get a bloody move on, you're already pushing it for time.'

9

ASHWORTH VILLAGE, WILTSHIRE, UK

Eight miles to the north-east of Mike Sampson's yard, in the scenic village of Ashworth, an airline pilot by the name of Tina Curtis was, at that very moment, woken by the intrusive jangling of her alarm clock.

She pulled her freshly laundered captain's uniform from its plastic dry-cleaning sleeve and quickly dressed.

She opened the bedroom curtains, allowing herself a brief moment to enjoy the understated beauty of the fields and trees which lay before her. Many of Tina's fellow pilots had thought her crazy when she had moved so far out of London with her husband, but no matter how much of a nightmare the hour and a half commute up the M4 to Heathrow, Tina still thought their decision the right one.

The kitchen was homely, with exposed oak beams and an oil fired Aga. Tina poured herself some granola and drank a bitter cup of unsweetened black coffee as she browsed the flight instructions she had been handed the previous day at the airport.

The flight was JA 463, a Jetlink Alliance Boeing 747 leaving Heathrow at ten minutes past midday for an estimated ten and a half hour journey to Seattle. Tina would need to check in to flight operations at least one and a half hours before the sector in order to complete the pre-flight regulations and paperwork.

Tina finished her breakfast and placed the Seattle dossier

back in her flight case. Then she went back upstairs to the bedroom to prepare her overnight bag.

10

SILSBURY VILLAGE, WILTSHIRE, UK

Mike Sampson drove Howard back to his house where the vet noticed immediately by the absence of MTV on the television that his thirteen-year-old son was most certainly not awake.

'Will?' he called up the stairs. 'You've got twenty minutes to get to school. I do *not* want you back on report again, you hear?'

There was no response. The vet raced up to Will's bedroom. 'Will! You've slept through your alarm. You've got five minutes to be dressed and out of that door.'

There was a vague grunt from beneath the duvet, the best communication Howard could hope for under the circumstances. 'I'm going up to Newbury with Mike Sampson,' he told the inert figure. 'You'll have to get yourself off to school. Five minutes, you hear?'

Will gave what sounded like an affirmative moan from beneath his duvet as Howard ran back downstairs and put out breakfast cereals and milk on the table.

The moment he slammed the door, Howard realized he'd left his keys on the table. He checked his pockets. 'Damn it. Hang on, Mike.' He bent to the letterbox and shouted through: 'Will! It's me. Open up, I forgot my keys.'

There was no reply. Howard stepped back and picked up a handful of gravel then threw it lightly at Will's bedroom window. 'Will! Let me in.' But there was still no response. Then he realized that Will could well be in the shower.

'Forget it,' he told Mike as he climbed into the BMW, 'Rebecca'll be back from work by the time we get back from Newbury. She'll let me in. We'd better hit the road.'

As the saloon turned out of the drive, Will pulled back the hallway curtain a fraction to watch it go.

In his hands were his father's keys.

11

EVEREST NORTH FACE, NEPAL

Back on Everest, Kuni placed her hand on the first of the holds. She hauled herself up, finding a fist-sized hole in the face in which she could jam the front spikes of her crampons. She brought her left leg up, balancing precariously on a tiny nodule of prominent rock, then jammed her left arm into the crack which ran up the corner of the cliff.

Two more moves and she was under the overhang.

This was the crux, the big swing up with the right hand, grasping onto the lip of a crumbling shelf and pulling up with every ounce of strength. Here the rock was featureless and smooth; Kuni knew the spikes of her crampons would find no purchase on the face, that her feet would be dangling over the vertigo-inducing drop, and that the slightest slip of her fingers would drop her into the void.

The young Japanese climber knew that five seasoned mountaineers had lost their lives attempting to climb this vertical wall of rotten rock and ice in the past year alone. Indeed, this was the place where those great Everest pioneers Mallory and Irvine had last been seen.

Kuni steeled herself, sucking deeply on the oxygen mask which covered her face, trying to force her atrophied muscles into action as her mind prepared her for the moment of commitment. Then with a powerful, fluid lunge she went into the move, her right hand slamming onto the little ledge above her head and taking the full weight of her body as she swung out from the crack.

A heartbeat later she felt her gloved hand beginning to slip, her frozen fingers scrabbling as her body swung over the void.

12

HINKLEY, WILTSHIRE, UK

Will's mate Jamie was cycling to school along the back alley behind the allotments when his mobile pinged off in his blazer pocket. He pulled out the Nokia and checked the display before taking the call.

'Hi, Will.'

'Where are you?'

Jamie wobbled out of the alley, unbalanced with the telephone pressed to his ear.

'Near school.'

'We're not going to school today. My dad left his keys behind.'

'I can't skive off today, I've got to hand my geography in.'

'Screw the geography. There's something you got to see.'

'What?'

Now Will was really insistent: 'Get round here.'

Jamie ended the call and watched the string of kids heading towards the school. A hollow feeling clutched at his gut. But he had to admit he was curious to know what his mate was so worked up about.

Cursing under his breath, Jamie mounted his bike, heading for the edge of town and the country lanes which led to Will's place.

Fifteen minutes later he turned into the driveway and stood his mountain bike against the wall. Will was standing in the doorway with a big smirk on his face.

'Check this out.' Will jangled a bunch of keys.

Jamie followed Will into his father's study. Jamie had been in the room before, but he'd never noticed the tall metal cabinet bolted to the wall.

'You know what this is?'

Jamie shrugged as Will inserted the key, the seven lever deadlock snapping back with a satisfying metallic clunk.

The two boys peered inside.

'Wow. That's wicked.' Now Jamie could see what his friend was getting at.

'Told you.'

13

ASHWORTH VILLAGE, WILTSHIRE, UK

Airline pilot Tina Curtis switched on Radio Four as she cruised through the village in her Audi TT, enjoying the sensual aroma of the leather-lined interior as she passed the immaculately tended cricket pitch and the war memorial.

As she drove, Tina found her thoughts turning to her husband who was at that moment working as a medic for the charity Africa Frontline Care in Malawi. Tina admired him for what he was doing, but a nagging part of her wondered if Martin's decision to take time out in Africa was a warning sign of other problems: they were both in their early forties, theirs was a marriage without the bonding effects of children (not that they hadn't tried), and maybe he had simply got tired of their quiet existence in the remote Wiltshire village which was their home. It wasn't a mid-life crisis, exactly, but it *was* a mid-life separation, and that worried Tina in a way which was hard to shrug off.

Traffic was heavy, and Tina found herself glancing frequently at the dashboard clock. It was 09.05a.m. already.

She piled up the revs, taking out a string of lesser mortals in their Mondeos and Minis as she accelerated to eighty-five, ninety miles an hour. She kept a wary eye for police patrol cars in the rear-view, slowing down to seventy as she passed the one speed camera on the road, then put in a finishing burst to beat a cattle truck as the dual carriageway petered out.

Tina knew it would give the airline problems if she was

late. The duty roster had been stretched recently by the number of pilots calling off sick and there was no doubt it would cause major scheduling problems if she missed the Seattle flight.

She *had* to be at Heathrow by ten forty. It was a question of professional pride.

14

SILSBURY VILLAGE, WILTSHIRE, UK

The gun was a Perazzi Custom, an elegant Italian-built twelve-bore shotgun with a twenty-nine inch barrel. It was a fine looking weapon, with a polished walnut stock, the silver-work scroll-engraved with game dogs and ducks in flight. Will pulled it away from the restraining clips inside the cabinet and cradled it in his arms before flashing Jamie a look.

'You ever shoot one of these?'

'My brother had an air rifle.'

'Yeah, but did you *shoot* it?'

'Once or twice.'

Will handed the gun over. Jamie raised it awkwardly to his shoulder.

'Jeez. Heavy, isn't it?'

He looked down the barrel, feeling his chest tighten with a burst of adrenaline.

'You get used to it.'

'Does your dad let you use it?'

Will laughed. 'You're kidding, right? He'd kill me first.'

'What if he comes back?'

'He's gone to a race. We got the whole day.'

Jamie sighted out of the window, finding the bird table in the centre of the garden. He lined up on a starling, the barrel shaking a little as the weight of the gun tested the muscles in his left arm.

'Kerbam.' Jamie let the gun snap back into his shoulder as he faked the shot.

'It hurts,' Will told him, snatching the gun back, 'when you do it for real.'

Will pulled a small cardboard box from the floor of the cabinet. He opened it, revealing a neat row of tightly packed red cartridges. Jamie could smell the sweetness of gunpowder and lead as he leaned to inspect the ammunition.

'Got to be a bit careful. We can't take too many.'

Will reached into the box of cartridges and pulled out a handful.

'So what are we going to do with it?' Jamie asked.

'We're going out to the chase. To kill something. And we're *not* talking squirrels.'

15

EVEREST NORTH FACE, NEPAL

Kuni slipped off her rucksack and sat heavily on the snow, taking out her flask and sipping some sweet, lukewarm tea as she thought back to the epic she had just experienced on the second step.

The second step. The closest she had ever been to sudden death. Her fingers searching for purchase on the loose shale and grit which was scattered about the ledge. How many seconds had it been before her left hand had shot up and got a grip? Two, or three? It had seemed an eternity.

The young Japanese climber had levered herself upwards, the steel points of her crampons striking sparks from the rock as she gained the vital metre or two of height. One last burst of strength and she had made it to the top of the rock face where she now took some precious time out, giving her mind a chance to recover from the terror of the near fall.

She checked her watch: the pressure was on. The day was getting late. It was time to continue towards the summit, threading a way along the narrow ridge line, in places no wider than her feet, with the awesome drop of the North Face on her right-hand side, and the even more terrifying fall of the eastern or Kanshung face on her left.

Kuni shivered as she sipped more tea, knowing that she had to get moving once again, despite the fact that her body was crying out for rest. She had to keep her focus on the summit, and the radio call to her father which would make him the proudest man in the world.

She packed away the flask and put the rucksack on her back. Then she took her ice axe in her right hand and kicked into the ice slope above her.

16

SILSBURY VILLAGE, WILTSHIRE, UK

Will and Jamie couldn't risk being seen. Two thirteen-year-old boys roaming wild on a school day would always attract attention; but if someone saw the gun, they might even call the police. So they mounted their bikes and took the quietest route to their destination, a circuitous journey which took them down a rutted farm track. The clandestine trail was a thrilling one, made even more so when they were forced to dive for cover as a tractor lumbered into view.

'If he sees us,' Will whispered as they crouched behind a musty stack of straw bales, 'I'll just shoot him.'

The tractor clattered past and a short time later the boys entered the gloomy fastness of the forest where they hid the bikes in some brambles. Jamie damaged both his hands in the task, emerging with a curse. He sucked the beads of blood from the scratches, wincing at the bitterness on his tongue.

'I hate the taste of blood.'

Will unzipped the gun case, pulling the gleaming weapon out with a flourish. He fumbled with the mechanism for a few seconds before finding the release which broke the barrel open. Then he inserted a cartridge into the breach and snapped the barrel back. He flipped the safety catch.

'Now we're armed. And dangerous.'

'Seriously dangerous.'

Will hid the gun case beside the bikes then turned to Jamie: 'I just thought of something.'

'What?'

'No one knows where we are. And no one knows we've got a gun. We could do anything with it.'

'Yeah. Go rob a bank. Take someone hostage.'

'I could shoot you, bury your body, and it'd be the perfect crime.' Will gave Jamie his best psycho look.

'Will?'

'What?'

'You're an idiot.'

The two boys went deeper into the woods.

17

MIKE SAMPSON'S YARD, WILTSHIRE, UK

For Keiron and Gary the clock was ticking. The two jockeys absolutely *had* to get to Newbury for the twelve thirty race and as a result they had packed up in record time, coaxing the horses inside the transporter with bribes of apples and swiftly loading up the tack and saddles they would need later that morning.

Keiron took the driver's seat as Gary slid a Megadeth CD into the dash player. They lurched out of the yard with the skull-pulverizing thrash metal anthem '*Killing is my business . . . and business is good!*' thumping out of the speakers at maximum volume.

From their high vantage point in the cab they could see for miles across the flat terrain. Far enough to notice a car moving at high speed along the road they would shortly be joining.

'That Audi's shifting like crazy!' Keiron exclaimed. 'Won't be so fast when I pull out in front of it!'

'No chance,' Gary told him dismissively. 'That'll be long gone by the time you get there.'

'A can of lager says I can beat it.'

Gary laughed. Was there *anything* that Keiron wouldn't put a bet on? 'You're on.'

Keiron kicked down hard on the accelerator, the rickety old horsebox rattling as it picked up speed on the rutted track. 'Warp speed!' Keiron whooped. Gary put his hands over his eyes in mock terror.

At the last moment the Audi seemed to accelerate. It looked as if the driver could see she might just beat the horsebox if she stepped on the gas. It was a small game of chicken, an attempt to force the horsebox driver to give way. But Keiron wasn't going to miss out on his can of lager, and he turned aggressively out onto the road in front of her.

18

SAUNCY WOOD, WILTSHIRE, UK

Jamie was the first to see the deer, grazing on fern shoots on the edge of a glade. It was a small buck muntjac with stubby black horns, nibbling nervously at the ground, stamping its hind legs occasionally against the flies. Jamie motioned to Will to get down, and the two boys crouched in slow motion behind a patch of nettles some fifty metres from the buck, barely daring to breathe.

'This is ace!' Jamie whispered, a big smile creasing his face.

'Told you you'd enjoy it.'

'Shhh!'

The deer raised its head, its neck craning as it warily sniffed the breeze. Will put his mouth close to Jamie's ear.

'We need to get closer,' he whispered, 'I won't get it from here.'

'It'll hear us.'

'Wait for a car. We're near the road.'

Jamie realized that Will was right. The road through the forest was quite close by. The tyre rumble of a passing vehicle might distract the deer. Three or four minutes later they got their opportunity. They inched forward commando style through the undergrowth, reaching a shallow dyke which would shelter them from the creature's line of sight.

'Got to keep completely quiet,' Will whispered again.

The two boys set out, crouching, trying not to crush

twigs beneath their trainers, picking the softer, quieter ground.

Much closer to their target, Will inched the barrel up over the edge of the dyke.

The deer was still there. Unaware it was being stalked.

19

THE A631, WILTSHIRE, UK

Tina had to brake hard to avoid a collision with the horsebox, sending her speed gauge plummeting down to thirty miles an hour as she sat in the noxious black smoke the old vehicle was churning out.

'Thanks a bunch,' she muttered bitterly, imagining the laughter in the cab from the two stable hands who had stuffed her. Certainly there was no chance to overtake such a vehicle now, the oncoming traffic would be solid to the M4.

Tina hated horseboxes, they were so damn *slow.*

Then her mind was running through the options. Eight miles to the motorway. And from there another hour to Heathrow—if it was clear. Time was already getting extremely tight and for that reason Tina decided she would take her special detour and try and beat the horsebox to the next roundabout. It was a game she sometimes played, shaving the odd second off her route, and this particular shortcut was a sport-driver's dream. 'Shortcut' wasn't really the word: the detour was actually about a mile and a half longer as it looped through a forest and along the side of one of the gallops.

But the road was quiet, and there were no speed cameras. It was the type of road that people like Tina use to have a little fun. The turning was next to a local landmark known as the Middelton folly, a distinctive, ruined tower standing alone in a field. As she reached the tower, Tina made a snap decision, steering the Audi off the highway and entering the narrow confines of the forest road.

20

SAUNCY WOOD, WILTSHIRE, UK

The deer stiffened suddenly, coming rigidly to attention as it scented something on the wind. Will could see the terror shine in its eyes as he levelled out the barrel and took aim. For one thrilling moment he actually had the creature in his sights, then, with a dazzling skip of acceleration, the deer was running and so were the boys.

'Don't lose him!' Will instructed. 'You go to the right!'

Jamie took the instruction, bearing away from the glade as he tried desperately to keep the deer in sight. Low-hanging branches whipped across his face as he sprinted at full pace through the forest, his ankles ripping through brambles, his arms beating back saplings as he stumbled and carried on. Jamie vaulted the rotting log of a fallen tree. Ahead of him, jinksing now to one side then the other, the panicking deer shot through the woods. Will was running parallel to him, the gun waving wildly in his hand.

Jamie felt his heart pounding with a primeval thud in his chest. The stick in his hand felt like a real weapon. Jamie had never felt like a killer, a hunter, but now he was in the business of hunting a creature down and nothing had ever felt so good.

21

GLASGOW AIRPORT, GLASGOW, UK

Kuni's father Ren was on one of his frequent business trips to the UK when he received the update call from base camp. It was 09:34a.m. UK time. At that moment he was sitting in a black cab, about to be dropped off at Glasgow Airport.

Kuni's father smiled broadly as he heard the hiss of the satellite connection from Nepal. He had been on tenterhooks all morning waiting for news from Everest.

'Mr Hayashi, this is Tony again at base camp.'

'How is my daughter doing?'

'Well, she made it up the second step.'

'How high is she? What time do you think she will reach the summit?' Hayashi had never doubted his daughter would make it.

'Last time we spoke to her she reckoned on another hour or perhaps more.'

Hayashi checked his watch, making a quick calculation. 'I'm in Glasgow, about to take the shuttle down to Heathrow. I'll be there in about an hour and a half. I won't be able to take her call while I'm on the plane. '

'I think that'll work out fine,' the base camp manager responded. 'She should reach the top about the same time you can switch your mobile back on. She's definitely going to want to be patched through to you, she's made that clear.'

'OK. Listen, when you next have a radio contact with her, give her all my love. I'm thinking of her every moment.'

Hayashi terminated the call and paid the taxi driver his

fare. As he hurried towards departures he wondered, not for the first time, if he had done the right thing in bankrolling the fifty thousand dollars it had cost to get Kuni on to the expedition. She was so ambitious, but what if something went wrong? Hayashi shivered a little with the thought.

His flight was already boarding. Ren rushed for the gate.

22

SAUNCY WOOD, WILTSHIRE, UK

There was no way she could avoid it. One moment the road was clear, Tina slipping the Audi into fifth gear, pushing the accelerator harder as she relished the taut response of the vehicle on the twisting forest road. The next the deer was leaping out into her path, thudding with a sickening impact into the front wing, its body tossed into the air for a split second before vanishing from sight.

Tina skidded to a halt. A few granules of broken glass pittered onto the bonnet. Wispy tufts of fawny brown fur floated down. There were droplets of blood on the windscreen. Out of the passenger window she could see the deer lying on the verge. It was a horrible sight, writhing in what looked like its death throes, blood running freely from an ugly gash in its flank, its eyes rolling with shock.

Tina checked her watch, thinking immediately of the Seattle flight and her tight time schedule. If the car was too damaged to drive she would have to get it to a garage, perhaps even get a taxi to Heathrow.

'Hell.' This really wasn't a good start to the day.

Feeling slightly nauseous with the shock of the event, she pulled the car into a safer position on the verge.

Tina stepped out and checked the damage: the headlight was smashed, the bodywork heavily dented, but to her relief it looked as if the car would be OK to drive. Over on the verge the deer was still moving, its legs pawing at the ground as it dragged itself forward on its knees. Tina looked at it in horror, willing the creature to die. But it did not. She took a few hesitant steps towards it, wondering what the hell she was going to do.

'You're all right,' she told the creature, trying to make her voice soothing but failing as it cracked with nerves. 'Everything's OK.'

23

LONDON, UK

Sixty miles to the east of Tina's position, in the London borough of Southwark, a six-year-old girl called Sophie was at that very instant ripping her way through a pile of birthday presents while her parents looked on with pride.

A number of smaller gifts had been explored but now it was time for the big one.

'Happy birthday, sweetheart!' Her father Dean watched, smiling, as Sophie pounced on her main present with glittering eyes. Seconds later, wrapping paper in shreds on the floor, she had the *Hannah Montana* karaoke microphone in her hands, singing along with delight as the opening chords of 'Pumpin' Up the Party' ripped through the morning calm.

Pleased with the success of the presents, Dean sat at the kitchen table, waiting for his morning fry-up and perusing the racing pages of *The Sun*.

'Are we still on for Six Lakes?' His wife Shelley looked out from the kitchen.

Dean sighed; much as he wanted to give his daughter a day she would remember at London's newest theme park, a day off work was a day's less pay when you were a self-employed plumber. 'I've got a lot of work on, Shell.'

'It's her birthday.'

Shelley put bacon, eggs and sausages in front of her husband. 'Pretty please.'

'Go on, Dad! I want to go on the Tormentor!'

'The *what?*'

'That new roller coaster. Don't you watch the ads?'

'Oh, all right.' Dean set to his breakfast, propping his copy of *The Sun* up against a ketchup bottle to check the runners of the day. Like many habitual gamblers, Dean normally went on instinct alone, the name of a horse or a rider more important to him than previous form. He found nothing of interest on the lists for Chepstow and Doncaster. So he turned his eye to the Newbury races.

24

SAUNCY WOOD, WILTSHIRE, UK

Tina looked up and down the road, wanting another vehicle to appear, but the forest was silent apart from the ragged breathing of the wounded deer. Suddenly, the creature made a rasping cry, a high-pitched croak frighteningly like the scream of a child.

Tina stepped closer, close enough that she could almost touch the injured animal. Now the deer was looking her in the eye, jerking with terror as she stood over it. Tina realized that it would blame her for the pain, would think that she was responsible. Tina felt tears prick. What to do? For a crazy moment she wondered if she should drag the poor thing so that its head was beneath her wheels—run over it to end the agony.

But she didn't want to touch it.

She went to the boot and retrieved the jack handle from the emergency tool kit. She tested the weight of it against her hand, feeling slightly foolish, as she wondered if a blow from the tool would put the deer out of its misery. The deer gave that same shrill, terrible cry, then half raised itself. Tina approached, causing the deer to scrabble ever more frantically to its feet.

Then it was up, legs flailing as it crashed wildly into the forest. 'Oh God.' Tina hesitated, wanting nothing more than to climb back into her car and put this horrible incident behind her. But how long would the deer last? It was clearly in agony and Tina couldn't bear the thought of that.

It might suffer for hours, she thought with a shudder, or even days before it died.

She had to put the creature out of its pain. Tina set off into the forest, following the trail of crushed leaves and blood which the wounded deer had left behind.

25

THE SHORES OF LAKE MALAWI, EAST AFRICA

At that exact moment, five thousand miles to the south-east, on the shores of Lake Malawi in Africa, a six-year-old boy stood waiting for a small fishing boat to land its catch. It was just after 11.45a.m. local time.

His name was Bakili, and he was thinking about nothing but the chance to beg some fish to ease his hunger pains.

Around him were forty or fifty other children, each clutching a small bowl, their hungry eyes locked on to the vessel as it chugged up to the sandy shore. Bakili had walked in his bare feet for almost an hour to be there.

The boat swung into shore, and the children could see from the glum expressions of the crew that their night had not been a productive one. The captain waved at the gang of children. 'Go home to your villages. We have nothing for you.' The children said nothing, but merely stood, expressionless. Then the captain relented. 'Go on,' he ordered one of the deckhands, 'give them that crate.'

The deckhand hoisted a plastic crate up from the deck and threw it onto the shore. A scrum erupted as the children dived for the miserable fish it contained. Bakili was weak, but he still fought valiantly for his share, squeezing through the ruck and managing to grasp one tiny fish, no longer than his little finger. He put it in his tin bowl and replaced the lid as the scramble subsided.

He thought about his family back in the village. They

would be bitterly disappointed when he returned with such a pathetic prize. He felt tears prick his eyes as he watched the boat crew light a fire to cook up some food.

26

SAUNCY WOOD, WILTSHIRE, UK

Jamie had run so hard he had stars before his eyes. He collapsed among the roots of a giant chestnut, gulping air into his lungs as a red-faced Will arrived by his side.

'Which way did it go?' Will asked.

Jamie wiped sweat out of his eyes. 'I don't know.'

'Well, you shouldn't have lost it, you idiot.'

'I never lost it . . .' Jamie protested, 'it was running in your direction.'

'You cut your face.'

Jamie raised his hand, felt the ridge of a congealing scab on his cheek where a branch had lashed him.

'Come on.' Will kicked at Jamie's ankle.

'Ow!'

Jamie raised himself awkwardly to his feet.

'Where are we, anyway?'

The two boys looked around them, realizing for the first time that the chase had left them disoriented.

'No idea. But I think it went over there.'

Still breathing hard, the two boys made their way through a dense thicket of beech for several minutes, emerging—to their surprise—to find themselves at the road.

'I thought the road was behind us.'

'Look.'

A short distance from where they stood, a silver car was parked facing away from them. The boys stepped quickly back into the shadows of the forest.

'What's that doing here?'

'I dunno. Broken down maybe.'

'You don't think someone's looking for us?'

'Nah.'

'I need a rest,' Jamie said. He slumped down into the leafy floor of the forest and scratched hard at the blotches on his face. Will sat down next to him, cradling the gun lovingly in his hands.

'Five minutes,' Will said, 'then we're back on the hunt.'

27

LONDON, UK

Dean was halfway through his breakfast, still considering his options for a bet, when a particular horse caught his eye.

'Look at that!' he exclaimed, pausing with a sausage in mid-air between mouth and plate. 'There's a horse called Sophie's Day running in the twelve thirty at Newbury.'

'So?' Shelley hated his gambling, and suspected her husband lost a lot more than he admitted.

'Well, it's obvious. 'Sbound to win on today of all days, isn't it.'

Shelley gave him a look, but she knew she couldn't stop him. As soon as his breakfast was polished off, Dean was off in his battered old Bedford Rascal van. 'I'll just go and get some fuel,' he told his wife. At the newsagent's he bought twenty Royals, treating himself to the first cigarette of the day as he waited for the Tote to open. Dean was well known at the bookies, the proprietor greeting him warmly as he unlocked the door.

Once inside, there was no hesitation, Dean wasn't a man to mess around when it came to a flutter. Once he'd decided on a horse, that was it. The only question then was, how much to wager? He checked his wallet, flicking a thumb through the wad of notes and pulling out five twenties. One of the good things about being a plumber (in fact he sometimes thought it was the *only* good thing) was the cash in hand.

Dean selected one of the stubby blue pens and wrote

'Sophie's Day' on the yellow slip, followed by the time and course. Then he took the slip over to the counter and slammed down the notes with a flourish.

'What's the odds?' he asked.

'Ten to one.'

'That'll be a grand then. You might as well give it me now.'

The bookmaker gave a wry smile as he stamped the slip in the timing machine. 'We'll see.'

28

SAUNCY WOOD, WILTSHIRE, UK

Will and Jamie rested for a while, crouched in the gloom as Will picked leaves and other bits of vegetation off his clothes. 'I could shoot the tyres on that car,' he said.

'I thought you said we were short of ammo.'

'Yeah well, if we're not going to get a deer, we've got to shoot *something*, haven't we?'

'We will get the deer. Let's keep searching.'

When they were sure no other car was coming, the boys crossed the road, crouching at a run, entering the forest on the far side and sticking side by side as they continued their search. The canopy above them was thicker now, with the dense foliage of fir trees blocking the light.

'Bingo!' Will knelt by a patch of disturbed ground. 'Deer droppings.'

Jamie looked at the brown pellets, shiny and hard against the peaty soil.

'Looks like rabbits to me.'

Crack. The unmistakable snap of a breaking twig had them frozen to the spot, hearts immediately racing again. It was followed by a rustle of branches from a large clump of rhododendron bushes to their left.

'Now we're talking,' Will whispered to Jamie, 'it's over there.'

Will shouldered the gun, stepping gingerly towards the sound.

29

THE SHORES OF LAKE MALAWI, EAST AFRICA

Reluctant to face the long walk home, Bakili waited there on the beach, watching wide-eyed as the crew of the boat lit their small fire and fried up some plump chambo—the best eating fish in the lake. They ate the charred fish with handfuls of nsima—ground-up corn meal—but failed to offer any to the children.

Bakili's mouth watered at the sight and smell of the food. It was weeks since he had eaten a proper meal and now he faced a long, hungry walk back to the village of Chinchewe where his mother and sick grandfather waited.

He opened the lid of the pot and looked at the measly little fish inside. It would barely provide a mouthful of nourishment.

Bakili turned away from the lake and walked quickly away, the soles of his bare feet registering the immense heat of the day. As he crossed the burning sand a four-wheel drive vehicle pulled up and an important looking white woman jumped out. He saw her talking to someone inside the vehicle for a while, then she approached him, a smile on her face.

'Do you speak English?' she asked him. Bakili nodded. 'Did you come here to try and get food?'

Bakili nodded again.

'Can we see what you have in the pan?'

Bakili raised the lid and was surprised when the woman reacted with pleasure.

'But this is perfect! Get the camera out, Renny, we'll do a piece about this poor kid.'

Moments later Bakili found a television camera pointed at his face, with the smiling face of the reporter next to it. 'My name is Maria,' she said, 'and you're going to be on television in America. Could you just take the lid off the pot for us one more time, please?'

30

SAUNCY WOOD, WILTSHIRE, UK

Will curled his finger round the trigger, every sense alert as the two boys crept towards the fringe of the bushes.

They heard more movement, used the rustling to disguise their own creeping progress. Then they were up against the wall of vegetation, staring intently into the shadowy interior. Jamie thought it looked spooky in there, like some sort of fairytale evil forest in miniature. The rhododendrons had created their own canopy and it was clear they could only enter if they crawled.

'We'll have to go in,' Will mouthed.

'I'll wait here,' Jamie told him.

'No you won't.'

Jamie frowned, unsure, then followed on as Will crouched down and squirmed into the thicket on his hands and knees, pushing the gun before him. They made a few metres of progress before Will motioned for Jamie to stop. The rustling noises of the creature had started again, only this time it seemed to be coming towards them. They could hear a snuffling. God, they were so close they could actually hear it breathe!

Jamie began to wish he was somewhere else.

Will eased the gun into position and squinted down the barrel, trying to keep the sight steady. For a second or two he felt faint, then he realized he had stopped breathing. He silently drew the air into his chest. Now he could see new texture amongst the leaves. He wished for more light; it was almost pitch black here in the heart of the rhododendrons. There! The creature was revealed, Will could see a dark patch of movement coming dead towards him.

Will tensed his finger, curled it hard around the trigger, bracing himself for the explosion. From this range, he thought exultantly, he really couldn't miss.

31

HEATHROW AIRPORT, LONDON

At the very moment Will's finger was tightening on the trigger, a middle-aged man arrived at Heathrow airport looking for a target of his own.

His name was Mick Vines and he was a professional thief; an airport specialist, rotating his activities between the airports that are within an easy train journey of central London.

His anonymous looks were perfect for the job: slightly stress-worn, in his late forties, weak blue eyes with greying hair swept across a thinning head, he had the type of bland features which are virtually impossible to recall. He could hang about for hours in a busy terminal and attract no attention at all.

Mick made good money from his airport work. Heathrow and Gatwick attract plenty of upper class passengers on their way to expensive Caribbean and American destinations, their handbags bulging with cash, credit cards and travellers' cheques. Often, their bags would be left unattended for that crucial split second which was all that Mick needed.

Mick knew his patch; he knew every security camera, every angle of observation, to the extent that he never targeted a punter in full view of a camera.

Now, Mick entered the terminal, his eyes busy as he scanned the hall for policemen or other security.

Mick ordered himself a cappuccino and a doughnut at a

food concession and had his breakfast while he kept a discreet eye open for opportunities. Then he opened his *Daily Mail*, turning to the financial pages to see how his share portfolio was doing.

Most of his shares were plummeting with the latest market crash. Mick frowned, wondering why he had ever been suckered into putting his hard-earned cash into the city; it really was daylight bloody robbery.

32

SAUNCY WOOD, WILTSHIRE, UK

Jamie could tell from the way Will's body had gone rigid that he was on the point of firing the weapon. He screwed up his eyes, turning his head as he anticipated the bang. And that was when he saw it, almost perfectly camouflaged against a heap of dead leaves.

'Will!' he hissed. 'Don't shoot.'

'Shhhh!' Will shrugged off Jamie's hand.

'Look over there!'

Will glanced at him, ready to let fly with a volley of whispered swear words, when he saw what Jamie was pointing to. Just a couple of metres away, a furry creature lay on its side. For a second Will thought it was a dog, but then he realized it was a deer. It had short stubby horns just like the one they had been hunting and they had crawled right past it without even seeing it.

'What the—?' Will forgot to whisper.

'Shoot it. Before it gets up!'

Will swung the gun round as the bushes seemed to explode into life. There was a monumental crashing from in front of them as something heavy moved away fast in a flurry of splintered branches. The two boys looked at each other, shocked at the speed things were happening.

'What the hell was that?' Jamie hissed.

The deer lying on the leaves did not move.

The crashing receded, leaving the two boys trembling.

'That didn't sound like an animal.' Jamie's imagination

was running wild with demons. 'It was like it was on two feet.'

'Two feet?' Will replied with an evil smile. 'Like a werewolf or something?'

Jamie started to move away. 'I'm going home,' he told Will, 'I'm done with this.'

33

WASHINGTON DC, USA

At that moment, three thousand six hundred miles away, on the other side of the Atlantic, a video editor by the name of Kev Grupper was waiting for a call from Malawi. It was 05.05a.m. local time. He was working deep in the basement news offices of *Video Report International*, right in the heart of Washington DC.

It had been a quiet night so far, with just two correspondent reports coming in on the satellite link. Kev's job was to edit the raw material and package it out for syndication to the many hundreds of TV news channels which paid by the second for their content. The job was fine. It was the hours that sucked—eleven p.m. to eight a.m., six days a week.

Now the telephone rang and Kev found he had Maria Coster on the line from Malawi. 'Hi, Kev, we've got a nice famine piece for you out here. Are you ready for the feed?'

Kev munched through a muffin as the report came in, watching dispassionately as Bakili's story was relayed expertly in pictures and words.

'What do you think?' she asked.

'Yeah. It's OK. I mean all that stuff with the little fish is nice and graphic. But it feels soft, like it needs a bit more punch to the story. I like the idea of additional background on the kid. Is he still with you?'

'He's gone back to his village.'

'Can you go and shoot there? Get more on his situation? I mean the family stuff.'

'I've had this crew up since dawn, Kev,' Maria snapped.

'I understand, Maria,' Kev told her. 'But I really need something more substantial. The world has famine fatigue. If I'm going to sell this piece I need something a bit harder. More emotional.'

34

SAUNCY WOOD, WILTSHIRE, UK

Will pulled Jamie back by the collar of his jacket. 'You're not going anywhere,' he told him. 'That crashing noise must have been the other deer. The one we've been hunting. I saw it. I think I saw it.'

Will was looking towards the inert figure lying on the leaves.

'We can save our ammo on that one. Looks like it's already dead.'

He crawled over to the deer. 'Gross!' Will flinched as he saw the gaping wound in the deer's flank, the marbled blue sheen of internal organs visible through a veil of blood. The smell was intoxicating, the feral sweat of an animal in fear mingled with the butcher shop sweetness of blood and tissue.

Jamie asked, 'Is it dead?'

Will looked closer, fascinated to see that the deer was in fact still—just—alive, its body quivering, its breathing shallow. 'Come and have a look.'

'No.' Jamie blundered out of the bushes and waited for Will to join him.

'What's wrong. You scared of a little deer?'

'Course not. What's wrong with it?'

'Something's ripped it open.'

'Like what?'

'Dunno.' Will mauled the air with a snarl as he took the piss. 'Zombie. Black Panther, who knows.'

Jamie felt his throat tighten with fear. He gulped, trying to sound casual. 'Let's get back. If we go now we can still make afternoon lessons.'

Will tutted impatiently and swung the gun round to point it straight between Jamie's eyes.

'I said we're not going back until we shoot something.'

Jamie pushed the weapon aside, his sweaty palms leaving a moist sheeny patch on the dull metal of the barrel.

'You're not supposed to point guns at people.'

'Yeah, well, there's lots of things we're not *supposed* to do,' Will replied contemptuously. 'Come on, we'll go and try somewhere else.'

35

THE B436 NEAR WINDSOR, UK

Birthday girl Sophie and her parents got caught in Heathrow traffic as they made their way the short distance to the Six Lakes theme park, Sophie jumping up and down impatiently in the front seat of the plumber's old van as they inched their way towards the gleaming metal rides that had been built around a series of reclaimed gravel pits. 'This is the worst part of these places,' Dean grumbled. 'What bloody genius put a theme park right next to a bloody airport anyway?'

'Don't complain,' Shelley told him. 'We're getting there.'

Finally they arrived at the car park, where an officious parking supervisor instructed Dean to park in Zone F. 'They always tell you to go to zone F,' Dean chuckled, taking the turn towards Zone A, 'but we'll try our luck a bit closer.'

Dean parked in the closest slot he could find to the theme park entrance and the family walked across the vast parking lot with Sophie skipping excitedly ahead. Aircraft from Heathrow thundered high above them as they went.

Dean bought a family ticket, watching the planes while he waited for his credit card to be authorized.

'Look at that, Soph!' he told his daughter. 'That's a jumbo!'

The little girl screwed up her face as she squinted into the sky at the lumbering aircraft. 'It's noisy,' she said, putting her hands over her ears. Dean got the ticket and the family passed through the automated turnstile into the theme park. 'Can I go on the Tormentor?' Sophie asked. The advertisements for the terrifying new roller coaster had been running all week.

'I don't know.' Dean winked at Shelley. 'Ask your mum.'

'Go on, Mum, I'm big enough now.'

'We'll see, sweetheart, we'll see.'

36

LAKE MALAWI, EAST AFRICA

Maria Coster was fighting her corner from Malawi as the satellite call continued:

'Listen, Kev, the crew are exhausted. We've been driving up and down the damn lake for hours. The cameraman's got some sort of stomach bug. I'm feeling faint myself from the heat and stuff. This crew is really in need of a break.'

'I know, I know,' came the reply. 'Just a minute, Maria—just a minute more stuff with the kid. Maybe his mother's starving in her bed, maybe his sister's got malaria. I don't know. It's just I know what the networks are going to say and . . .'

'How about the shots I wired in yesterday? The stuff with the dead livestock, withered crops and so on.'

'I used it,' Kev snapped.

Maria sighed, resigned to her fate. 'All right, Kev, you win. We'll go check out his village. I'll file again later. Bye for now.'

Maria terminated the satellite call and turned to her crew who had been listening in on the conversation with jaded expressions.

'Same old, same old,' Maria told them. 'The guy at the end of the phone always wants more.'

The crew weren't happy about it but they climbed back into the vehicle with Maria and the Land Rover headed off up the road. Now, Maria thought, how the heck are we going to find this village? She unfolded her map and looked for the name that Bakili had told her but it wasn't even marked.

'Do you know where Chinchewe is?' she asked the driver.

The man shook his head. Maria's heart sank yet further. This was going to be a very long day.

37

MOTORWAY SERVICES, M4, BERKSHIRE, UK

Tina turned off the motorway into the service area and parked up outside the pyramidal glass frontage of the food hall. Normally she avoided motorway services like the plague but right now she really had to sort herself out.

For the hundredth time she cursed the stupidities of the morning. Whatever had possessed her to go after that wounded deer? It was only a bloody animal, for God's sake. And to think that she was trying to kill it, heading into the forest like that with a jack handle as a weapon; the whole thing was just too absurd for words. And then that weird incident in the thickest part of the forest, just as she had closed in on the wounded animal.

Voices.

Now that really was spooky. That was when she'd run. Surely there can't have been anyone in those bushes? Reason told her not but the only other answer was that the deer had somehow let out a noise that she'd mistaken. Whatever, the incident had scared her half to death, left her racing madly back to the car, her spine tingling from some nameless threat.

All damage to the car forgotten, she had burned rubber in her desperation to get away from that place, had driven like the wind back to the A road where she was amazed to find that the rest of the world was proceeding very much as normal.

Now, she checked her watch, making a quick mental

calculation of her chances of getting to Heathrow for the flight. It was clear that she could no longer guarantee to make it. The incident with the deer had lost her a good half an hour in the forest.

Tina took out her mobile and dialled the number for the flight control centre.

The number was engaged. Tina cursed and dialled again.

38

CHAMPLAIN, WASHINGTON DC, USA

As the clock ticked over 10.15a.m. in the UK, it was precisely 05.15a.m. in Washington. At an hour when most sane people are asleep, a man by the name of Shelton Marriner sat on the edge of his bed and decided that this would be the day he would die.

He was in his farmhouse, a neglected, rat infested mess of a place close to the town of Champlain and the Rappahannock river. He was midway through his fourth consecutive night without sleep.

He'd see his sons first. Then that would be the end.

The boys would have to die, of course, and that traitor of an ex-wife who had tried to get him sectioned into a mental institution after he'd had the first breakdown. Shelton had paid a private detective to track them down; he had been staring at the slip of paper with their address on it all through the night.

Shelton yawned, tired to his bones, more tired even than he'd been when he'd got back from the first Gulf war, poisoned in body and mind by the horrors he had witnessed.

Shelton pulled back the curtain a little, gazing with bloodshot eyes out from the darkened room into the forest of pine which surrounded the lonely house. For long minutes he stared into the darkest shadows, looking for a tell-tale sign, a glint of a weapon or the red glow of a careless cigarette.

The enemy was out there. Of that he had no doubt. He had

seen the markings on the trees. It could be his wife's new partner, the one who had called Shelton a 'joker' in the court proceedings. Mr Happy Families, Shelton called him.

He wouldn't be Mr Happy Families for much longer, Shelton thought. Because now it was time to prepare the bomb.

39

CHINCHEWE VILLAGE, MALAWI, EAST AFRICA

Bakili turned off the road and walked down the dusty track which led to the village of Chinchewe.

The family house was a modest one, handbuilt from sun-fired clay bricks with a rusting corrugated sheet of iron for a roof. Inside, Bakili's mother was tending to a small, smoky fire. A pot of water boiled on it but it contained no corn.

'Have you brought us fish?' his grandfather asked.

'No.' Bakili smiled triumphantly, 'I have money.'

Bakili's family looked at the hundred kwacha note in astonishment.

'A white lady talked to me with a camera. Then she gave me this.'

'Then we will eat well tonight,' his mother told him with a smile, 'I'll go to the market later.' She tucked the precious note into a fold of her dress.

'What about the fish?' the grandfather repeated.

Bakili opened the lid of the pot.

'They have taken too much from that lake,' the old man muttered, eyeing the small sprat with disgust. 'When I was a child it was teeming with fish as thick as your arm.'

'It is not the lake that worries me,' Bakili's mother said, 'it is the crops.'

'Without rain?' the old man spat. 'There will be no crops.'

Now his mother told him:

'Bakili, you must go to guard the field. Your brother has been out there all night.'

Bakili's heart sank. He hated to guard the field, mainly because he was terrified of the baboon packs which regularly raided the crops. Some of the creatures were bigger than he was.

'Go now,' his mother ordered, 'and tell Kamuzu to come straight back to me here. I need him to go for firewood.'

Bakili trod the path of his ancestors, heading for the high ground above the village.

40

NEWBURY RACECOURSE, BERKSHIRE, UK

Keiron and Gary turned the horsebox into the competitors' parking area at Newbury and took one of the last available slots. The majority of horses were already out and exercised and the two jockeys knew they would have to move fast to get Mazarine Town fully ready for the eleven o'clock inspection which would qualify her for the twelve thirty race.

'You guys oversleep this morning?' a fellow jockey called out from the back of his horse. 'You'll have to be sharper than that if you want to beat me.'

'Watch your own business,' Keiron told him with a smile, 'and don't worry about the twelve thirty. All you'll see is my candy arse.'

The two jockeys unlatched the tailgate, and lowered the ramp so that Mazarine Town and Beaumont Boy could be walked down onto the paddock. Both horses were good travellers, unfazed by the journey; their ears pricked as they saw the bustle around them.

Gary went to the tack box at the rear of the wagon while Keiron held the two horses. He took a careful look at the way Mazarine Town was standing but could see no sign that she was favouring either leg.

As they saddled up the horses, Mike Sampson's BMW pulled up beside them, the vet in the passenger seat. 'We'll have a last look at Maz,' Mike told the jockeys. 'I want to see her at speed. Just to be sure.'

41

CHINCHEWE VILLAGE, MALAWI, EAST AFRICA

Bakili headed up the dusty trail, making for the maize fields where he would find his brother. He was pleased that he had been able to give his family that one hundred kwacha note but any sense of pride was quickly extinguished by his mounting fear as he got further from home.

It was a lonely walk. There were few people around: the famine had driven most of the villagers away to the capital Lilongwe, where food aid programmes were keeping them alive. Now the only people left were those who were too sick or too old to be moved.

Bakili's own father had quit the village to try and find work in the capital city Lilongwe. His father had promised he would send back food or money; but so far—in the six weeks or so that he had been gone—they had heard nothing.

Bakili held his nose as he passed the wasteground where the villagers dumped the carcasses of dead cattle. The famine had the land in an unrelenting grip and the stench of decomposing animal corpses filled the air. The early season rains had failed completely, the skies clear and cloudless for week after week despite the prayers of the people.

Far ahead he thought he heard a noise. The distinctive grunt of baboons on the cliffs above the fields.

A sharp stab of fear ran through the six-year-old child as he heard it.

Baboons were the enemy. He had learned that long ago.

42

MOTORWAY SERVICES, M4, BERKSHIRE, UK

Tina got her line through to the flight controllers on the third attempt. 'Operations, good morning. This is Ross Hawker.' Tina was grateful. At least she had got one of the controllers who knew her personally. 'Oh hi, Ross, this is Tina Curtis. I'm afraid I've had to sort out a problem with my car this morning and I'm not going to make the Seattle flight.'

'We're having a hell of a morning here, Tina, we've had crew calling in sick, late, aircraft out of service, you name it. What time do you reckon you can definitely get here?'

'Eleven forty-five?' she told him. 'Depends on the traffic.'

'OK. It's a bit early to tell you what we'll transfer you on to. Report to the operations centre when you arrive and we'll let you know.'

Tina terminated the call and looked in the mirror. A nasty weal of blistered red tissue had sprung up beneath her eye and the subtle make-up which she had applied back at home was now looking decidedly the worse for wear.

She would have to clean up. Tina took her flight bag out of the boot and headed for the restaurant block. She entered the ladies' restroom and re-applied her make-up. As for her uniform, Tina didn't like what she saw in the full length mirror: her shoes were scuffed, her trousers stained with mildew from the forest. She cleaned off the worst of the blotches from her uniform with some tissue, and ran a brush through her hair.

'OK.' Tina took a deep breath, consciously trying to calm herself down. 'You're all right. Everything's OK.' She stopped, chilled, as she realized the words and tone were the same that she had used when trying to calm the wounded deer. God, this is a weird day, she thought, what the hell is going on?

43

NEWBURY RACECOURSE, BERKSHIRE, UK

Keiron mounted Mazarine Town and they walked her out to the training gallop which stood to the west of the main stand.

'Give her a good run,' the owner told him, 'but not so she's knackered for the race.'

Keiron did as instructed, letting her warm up for a few minutes, then putting in a two furlong gallop—not flat out but fast enough to put her to the test.

'What do you reckon, Howard?' Sampson asked the vet as the horse flashed past them.

'She's ninety-nine per cent there,' the vet told him, 'but I still couldn't swear she's completely sound. If you look at the way she picks up that left leg it just doesn't look quite right.'

'The tendon?'

'Maybe. But if it's a strain it might ease as she warms up.'

'And if it's a tear?'

'Just no way of saying. Not without that scan.'

'Bring her over!' the owner called to Keiron.

The vet ran his hands over the horse's leg once more. 'There's the smallest hint of a bump in there,' he said, 'but if it's a torn tendon it's giving her remarkably little trouble.'

'She looks well enough in herself,' the owner added, 'her eyes are bright and she looks keen.'

'She'll do,' pronounced the vet. 'It's a one per cent risk, but . . . ?'

Mike Sampson slapped the horse on the flank. 'One per

cent? Hell, we wouldn't be in this game if we couldn't live with a little risk now and then. We'll go for it. Get yourself to the weighing room, Keiron, we'll keep her in the race.'

Keiron dismounted and the owner helped him to unfasten the saddle. Then, saddle in hand, the jockey walked off to the weighing room, pleased that the race was still on.

44

CHINCHEWE VILLAGE, MALAWI

Bakili's brother Kamuzu was tired. He had spent the entire night guarding the field and was longing for his younger brother to come and relieve him. Of all the duties the two brothers shared, the necessity to protect their few remaining maize plants from thieves was easily the most important . . . and also the most demanding.

Since the famine had struck, there had been a big increase in the amount of casual pilfering and a moment's inattention could cost the family their meagre crop. There were plenty of scavenging animals too, the worst being the marauding baboons which lived among the rocky cliffs. The famine had struck the creatures hard, and as they, like the local villagers, had begun to starve they had become bolder.

Day by day their raids on the fields had become more brazen, more desperate.

In the past, Kamuzu could easily scare the baboon pack away by shouting and waving his stick. As soon as he heard the crack of breaking stalks, Kamuzu would rush into the standing corn, yelling, whistling and beating his stake against the ground. The baboons would scream back, scattering in all directions and rushing out of the field to chatter and taunt from a distance.

One of the baboons had given Kamuzu particular cause for concern—baring his teeth and letting Kamuzu get extremely close before he reluctantly dropped his stolen maize cobs and fled. It was almost as if his hunger had caused the creature to lose his natural fear of man, Kamuzu thought, and it was the biggest male of the pack.

The alpha male. Kamuzu had learned the term at his school, and he had a hunch that the cantankerous monkey was the alpha male. He hated that creature. And he was pretty sure that the feeling was mutual.

45

CHAMPLAIN, WASHINGTON DC, USA

Shelton left the bedroom and padded down the stairs. He picked his way through the unwashed crockery and half-eaten TV dinners which littered the floor and quietly opened the internal door to the garage. He switched on the light and opened the rear doors to the fifteen-year-old Chevrolet van, a recent purchase bought specifically for the task at hand. He'd oiled the hinges so the doors wouldn't make a sound.

The load bay of the van was empty, the corrugated steel of the floor streaked with rust and corrosion. Shelton crossed to the corner of the garage and pulled away a tarpaulin to reveal a big stack of twenty kilo bags.

Inside the bags was Ammonium Nitrate, a widely used fertilizer that Shelton had been buying, little by little, over the previous months. Internet research had taught him how to turn this seemingly innocuous powder into a potent bomb by mixing it with a few basic ingredients and igniting it with a detonator. He had tested the recipe out with some small scale explosions in the woods and was well satisfied with the results.

Now it was time for the big one, Shelton thought with some relish as he viewed the pile of fertilizer; this one's really going to raise some hell.

He began to lug the sacks across to the van.

46

FLIGHT OPERATIONS CENTRE, HEATHROW AIRPORT

Flight operations manager Ross Hawker called in two of his colleagues for a situation report at the Heathrow HQ of Jetlink Alliance.

'We just got another late show,' Hawker told his colleagues. 'Captain Curtis can't make it in time for the Seattle Four Six Three. Do we have any more flight crew on standby?'

'They're all on sick cover.'

'Nightmare. Now how are we going to crew that flight?'

The three operators stared at the vast wall chart, looking for the logical route through the impasse.

'How about we re-shuffle the crew off the Rome Six Nine Two? Tina Curtis could take it out with a one hour delay and we could re-roster them onto the Four Six Three. How's the Rome flight looking?'

'Heavy,' the assistant told him. 'One hundred and sixteen pax. Business class full.'

Hawker turned back to the chart; it was not company procedure to purposely delay a flight with a full business section.

'Looks to me like there's only one route through this one,' Ross told the others as he moved a name card up the ladder. 'We put Brian Millican onto the Seattle flight to replace Tina Curtis.'

'Which leaves the eleven thirty Edinburgh shuttle without a crew.'

'What's the loading on the Edinburgh One One Six?' Ross asked.

'Light. Thirty-one pax.'

'Can we consolidate with the next flight?'

'Comfortably.'

'OK. Then we cancel it and consolidate with the One One Eight. Job done.'

'OK. Edinburgh cancelled. And Captain Curtis?'

Hawker picked up Tina's name designator and viewed the chart.

'Captain Curtis, comrades, is on her way to Moscow.'

47

NEAR LAKE MALAWI, AFRICA

Maria Coster and her film crew found a petrol station not far from the lake where they could fill up with fuel and ask for directions to Bakili's village. 'We're looking for Chinchewe,' Maria told the attendant, her hopes not exactly raised by the baffled look that the name inspired.

The attendant went away for a long and involved conversation with a colleague then came back and drew them a map in pencil on the back of an envelope, a hastily scribbled maze of intricate lines which to Maria's eyes looked more like a drunken spider's web than an accurate guide.

Nevertheless they had to do their best. They left the tarmac road and began to negotiate a dusty track which was littered with sharp rocks.

And that was when they got the puncture, an ugly jagged rip in the sidewall of one of the front tyres which was quite clearly more than they could repair on the spot.

'Do we have a spare?' Maria asked the driver.

'We took it out this morning so we could get the satellite gear in.'

Maria cursed. It was true that their bulky satellite equipment had left no room for the extra tyre.

'So what can we do?' she asked, despairing as she thought of the deadline to send more material back to Kev in Washington.

'I can walk back to the road and go for a mechanic,' the

driver suggested helpfully. Maria and her film crew sat, baking, in the stifling heat of the vehicle as they watched the driver walk slowly away into the heat haze.

48

EVEREST SUMMIT, NEPAL

Kuni took the final step. It was almost 5p.m. local time. She was standing on the summit of Everest with the entire range of the Himalayas stretched out beneath her. She let her eyes feast, exulting in the view her young heart had longed for, recognizing summits like Machupuchare, Shishapangma, and—far away to the east—the lonely massif of Kanchenjunga. She raised her ice axe in the air and gave an intense scream of pleasure before sitting beside the aluminium summit pole and taking out her walkie-talkie. 'Kuni to base camp.'

'Hey, Kuni, we've just seen you through the telescope. Congratulations from everyone here; everyone's singing and dancing round the mess tent! How are you feeling?'

'Relieved,' Kuni told him, 'and very tired.'

'Any problems on the last section?'

'Plenty. I don't like the final ice slope. It's too steep!'

'Yeah but you made it and that's what counts.'

'What about my father? Can you connect me now?'

'Yeah. I'll have to break this connection for a couple of minutes, but stand by and we'll see if we can do that. I spoke to him earlier on without any problems. Stand by, OK?'

'OK.' Kuni heard the characteristic click as the radio went dead. For a moment she stood, still marvelling at the view, thinking how privileged she was to be witnessing it and then thinking with a surge of pleasure how deeply proud her father would be.

The radio squawked back into life: 'Kuni, this is base, I'm afraid we're having a bit of trouble getting through to your father in the UK.'

'What's wrong?'

'We're getting his answerphone. He did say he was taking a short internal flight but he should be available any minute.'

'Keep calling him. I need to speak to him here on the summit! Please keep dialling.'

'Roger. Stand by and we'll try again.'

49

FIELDS ABOVE CHINCHEWE VILLAGE, MALAWI, EAST AFRICA

Kamuzu was exhausted. He had spent more than twelve hours wrapped up in a blanket on the small wooden platform which acted as a look-out post, only descending to scare away the baboons or to tend to the little fire he kept for comfort. He kept glancing down to the valley floor, yearning for the sight of Bakili coming along the trail to take over the job.

But there was no sign of his younger brother.

Then he heard a squabble amongst the baboons, followed by silence and then the distinctive crunching of maize stalks. Kamuzu got quickly to his feet, standing on his toes to determine where the raid was happening. Then he hollered loudly, uttering a series of high pitched cries in the hope of scaring the animals as he rushed into the maize with his stick.

Kamuzu rushed through the tall maize, whistling and yelling at the top of his young voice. He could see no more than a couple of metres ahead, but he could hear the sound of the scavengers ripping into the crop and he used the noise to orientate himself.

There.

The baboons were right in front. Kamuzu burst through the maize and slammed his stick hard against the ground just an arm's length from the nearest animal. He could see it was the big one—the alpha male—and normally he would expect the creature to run. But the baboon did not run. In fact it did the very last thing that Kamuzu expected.

The baboon attacked him with its fangs fully bared, rushing beneath Kamuzu's upraised stick and delivering a savage bite to the child's inside thigh.

50

ON BOARD VIRGIN ATLANTIC FLIGHT VS040

Five thousand feet above London, an American Air Force officer by the name of Calder Lawton was enjoying the early morning view of the East End as the Virgin Atlantic Boeing 747 banked over the Millennium Dome and began its final approach to Heathrow.

The overnight flight from his home city of Chicago had been a pleasant one, the business class seat enabling Calder to get a few hours' rest as the red-eye express powered eastwards over the ice-bound wastelands of Greenland and the storm tossed waters of the North Atlantic.

Next to him was an elderly woman traveller, a grandmother on her way to visit her family in London.

'What do you do, young man?' she had asked as they had left Chicago.

'I'm a navy pilot, ma'am,' Calder had told her, which was at least half the truth.

In fact Calder Lawton was a trainee astronaut, seconded to Nasa from his duties as a Naval Air Squadron test pilot, one of just six black Americans on the American Space Program.

After a short layover at Heathrow he would be connecting to a Moscow flight and joining a joint US–Soviet training operation at Space City.

The aircraft landed smoothly at Heathrow. Calder bade a polite farewell to the elderly lady, who had snored into his ear throughout the night, and walked off the aircraft into the terminal, pleased to be halfway through his journey. He checked his watch, wondering if he had time to do a little shopping before his Moscow flight. Calder took the moving walkway, heading for the transit desk.

51

FIELDS ABOVE CHINCHEWE VILLAGE, MALAWI, EAST AFRICA

Kamuzu was so shocked that for a moment he just stood there, completely frozen to the spot, as warm blood began to gush from his groin, staining his shorts and running down the back of his leg. The huge baboon spun away, jabbering excitedly as it joined the other members of the pack a short distance away.

Kamuzu pulled back the fabric of his shorts, feeling instantly faint as he saw the deep wound. Blood was not just welling from it—it was positively gushing, and Kamuzu knew enough about the biology of the human body to know that the creature had punctured something important and that he was in imminent danger of bleeding to death.

'Hah!' he screamed at the baboons, brandishing the stave once more, desperate that they should not take the sight of so much blood as a cue to attack him as a pack. The creatures responded with threatening calls but for the moment they were too busy fighting amongst themselves to pay Kamuzu much attention.

Kamuzu felt his breaths coming too fast, his vision beginning to fill with stars. What to do? The attack had been so sudden—and so unexpected—that his young mind was reeling. What about his brother? Maybe he was even now at the look-out platform. 'Bakili!' he cried. 'Come quickly!' But there was no reply.

Kamuzu began to stagger slowly backwards, removing his T-shirt and pressing the garment against the wound to try and staunch the flow of blood. Soon he had lost sight of the baboons, making it to the path which led down to the valley. By then the T-shirt was drenched with his blood, and Kamuzu knew that he could not stay at the field—he had to go for help. And still the blood came from the wound, the strength of the spurts terrifying him as he watched his life ebbing away.

Then he was crawling, and the road was in sight.

52

SAUNCY WOOD, WILTSHIRE, UK

'I'm thirsty, let's go home,' Jamie complained, hating the gloomy forest and the hopeless quest for deer. For ages now they had seen nothing more exciting than the odd blackbird, and even they moved too fast to shoot.

Will checked his digital watch. 'It's still early, we've got hours before my dad gets back.'

'Yeah, but I really, really need a drink.' Jamie's mouth felt as if he'd swallowed a bag of chalk, his saliva unpleasantly thick.

'We could get the bikes and go over to St Ashborn, get a Coke at the post office,' Will suggested.

'What about the gun?'

'We'll hide it.'

'That's miles away, my legs are knackered as it is.'

Jamie sat heavily on the forest floor, blinking as annoying trickles of sweat ran into his eyes. Tiny midges emerged from nowhere, swarming around him until he could feel their sharp bites on his hands and neck.

'Tell you what,' Will told him, realizing that he had to do something to rouse Jamie from his apathy, 'we'll go back to the road and shoot a sign.'

Jamie perked up. 'What sort of sign?'

'You know, the ones with the picture of the deer crossing. There's loads of them.'

Jamie scrambled back onto his feet, his interest fired up. 'Will the bullets go through it?' he asked.

'You bet they will. They'll blow the holy crap out of it.'

Will chuckled as he led the way back to the road, relishing the thought of the impending target practice and wondering why he hadn't come up with the idea earlier.

Five minutes or so up the road they came to a thirty mile an hour limit sign.

'I thought you said they were deer signs,' Jamie moaned, feeling that the idea of shooting this one was somehow less sporting.

'What's the difference?' Will demanded. 'I'll still take it out anyway.'

53

ON BOARD BA225, HEATHROW AIRPORT

Ren Hayashi's flight from Glasgow to Heathrow had landed bang on schedule, the one hour sector barely giving the cabin crew time to serve teas and coffees before the Boeing 737 went into the descent to Heathrow.

Now, with the plane safely on the ground, the Japanese executive was sitting in his seat, wondering, along with the rest of the passengers, why the aircraft hadn't taxied to its gate. He was itching to turn on his mobile.

Suddenly the intercom crackled into life:

'This is the captain. I just want to give you an update on our situation here. You've probably noticed that we haven't moved in the last few minutes. The aircraft which was due to free up a gate for us was bound for Edinburgh but that flight's been cancelled. So we're now waiting for a gate re-allocation. I'm sure you appreciate that the airport is extremely busy today so there's not much I can do to hurry things along. As soon as we get any more news I'll be letting you know.'

Ren checked his watch, working out that it would be past five p.m. in Nepal. Then he pressed the call button to get the attention of a stewardess.

'Yes, sir?'

'Can I switch my mobile on?'

'I'm afraid not, sir.'

'But I'm expecting a very important call.'

The stewardess gave the Japanese executive her most brilliant smile.

'I appreciate that, sir, but even though we're not airborne you still have to keep all electronic items turned off.'

Of all the bad luck, he thought, fuming inside. His daughter would be delayed on the very summit of Mount Everest just because some lousy flight five thousand miles away had been cancelled.

54

CHINCHEWE VILLAGE, MALAWI, EAST AFRICA

Bakili could see something on the path in front of him. From a distance he thought it might be the body of a dead dog or goat. Then he saw it was his brother Kamuzu, the earth around him stained with his blood.

'Kamuzu!' he cried in horror. 'What happened? What have you done?'

Bakili raised his brother's head, relieved to see that he was still alive and that his eyes could focus.

'A baboon,' Kamuzu told him in a whisper, 'look.'

Bakili flinched as he saw the ugly wound on his brother's thigh.

'Help me to stop the blood,' Kamuzu told him weakly.

Bakili pressed the blood-stained T-shirt harder against the wound but he knew instinctively that his brother would die if he stayed here.

'Come on. Get up. You can't stay here.' Bakili put his arms beneath Kamuzu's shoulders and managed to lift him to his feet.

Then he crouched and took Kamuzu's weight onto his back, the load almost making his young legs buckle as he lifted him. He started to make his way back down the hill, his brother's arms wrapped weakly round his neck, knowing that the only chance would be to piggyback him to the road which snaked through the bottom of the valley. From there it was a short ride to the nearest clinic where he might be saved.

If they were lucky enough to find a car or truck to take them.

The distance was not great but the load was unbearably heavy for Bakili and twice he had to stop for a rest, lowering his brother gently on to the ground from his back each time and calling to him urgently as he faded in and out of consciousness. 'Kamuzu? Kamuzu! Speak to me.' But his brother had blacked out, the blood loss sending his young body into deep trauma. Bakili got him up again, kept moving towards the road.

55

EVEREST SUMMIT, NEPAL

'Kuni to base camp. Did you get my father yet?'

'Negative. All we have is his answerphone, his mobile is still turned off.'

Kuni was dismayed. 'Keep trying,' she urged, 'I'm sure he will answer.'

'How much longer can you stay up there, Kuni?'

'I'll stay as long as I can. I can see two climbers coming up to the summit now, so at least I'll have some company.'

'Yeah, we can see them on the binoculars; we think it's two of the German team. Give them our love, OK?'

The two German climbers, Josef Theilart and Bernard Karl, reached the summit some ten minutes later, smiling with delight and embracing Kuni in their moment of triumph. Kuni knew them quite well from base camp and was happy to have some human contact. She took Josef's video camera and filmed the two of them for their sponsors, then took some stills.

Bernard returned the favour, spending a good few minutes taking a wide range of shots of Kuni.

'We're heading down now,' Josef told her. 'You want to come with us?'

'No thanks. I'm still waiting to try and speak to my father. I always speak to him on the summit when I climb.'

'Up to you. But don't push your luck, OK?'

Kuni embraced the two Germans, and watched as they began their slow descent, suddenly feeling very lonely and isolated. The day, which had so far been warm by Himalayan standards, was beginning to chill.

'Kuni to base camp. Any luck?'

'Not so far. Maybe his flight got delayed.'

'Five more minutes, then I have to go.'

'OK. Roger and out.'

Kuni pulled her wind suit closer round her, adjusting her hood so the fabric was close against her face. Where was her father? It was so unlike him to miss something like this.

56

CHAMPLAIN, WASHINGTON DC, USA

Shelton was halfway through loading the fertilizer, methodically hauling the heavy sacks across to the rear of the van and stacking them one by one along the side walls of the interior. When the side walls were done, he began to build a layer across the bed of the van floor, stacking a solid mass more than a metre deep, enough to cause the van's springs to creak with the pressure as the suspension compacted beneath the weight.

A noise. A sudden clattering from outside.

Shelton switched off his headtorch and waited, heart pounding, to see if the noise came back.

Now would be the perfect time for the enemy to strike.

Shelton peered out of the grimy window, noticing that the first glimmer of dawn was now visible to the east. For long minutes he stared keenly out into the forest, alert to any movement which would betray an observer. But all remained quiet. Shelton decided the clattering had probably been from the waste bins, some vermin rooting around for scraps. He turned the headtorch back on, nodding with satisfaction at the neat pile of fertilizer. Then he pulled a second tarpaulin off a further pile, revealing a stack of jerrycans, each one filled with twenty litres of fuel.

Shelton picked the top can off the pile and lugged it across to the van.

57

CHINCHEWE VILLAGE, MALAWI, EAST AFRICA

Bakili was still staggering down the track with his brother on his back when he heard the roar of an engine in the distance. A vehicle. He had to stop it.

He carried his older brother down to the road, lurching onto the laterite surface just as the four-wheel drive Toyota swept past. For a second it looked as if the driver would not stop, but then he slammed on the brakes and reversed back to the two boys.

'What's going on?' he asked through the window. Bakili recognized the driver, he was one of the workers at a nearby papaya plantation. Bakili was too shy to speak.

'Has he been in a fight?' The driver got out and took the almost inert body from Bakili.

'He was bitten by an baboon.'

'Don't say crazy things.'

Then the driver took a closer look at the wound. 'It does look like a bite,' he conceded. 'I can take him to the clinic. Where do you live?'

Bakili pointed to the nearby village as the driver placed Kamuzu gently on the back seat.

'Get in,' the driver told him. Bakili blinked, thinking through the situation. Every instinct told him to stay with his wounded brother to try and care for him. Also, he knew the baboons would be worse than ever now they had drawn blood. Bakili had always feared them—more even than Kamuzu—and the last thing he wanted to do now was to climb the hill to that lonely field. But he also knew his duty—and he knew that his family would starve without the precious maize.

'I cannot,' the child said, 'I have to go to the field. If I leave it the monkeys will take all we have.'

'Suit yourself. I'll go and ask for your mother in the village.' The driver got back into the car and drove away. Bakili picked up his brother's stick and began the climb up the hillside, his heart filled with dread.

58

SAUNCY WOOD, WILTSHIRE, UK

Will snatched the gun up, and let the stock nestle into his shoulder. He took careful aim from a stance about three metres from the target.

'You can't miss it from there,' Jamie scoffed, 'that's way too easy.'

'All right,' Will snapped, clearly riled. He took a few paces back and pointed the Perazzi at the signpost once more, closing his right eye and squinting along the barrel.

The recoil was brutal. Much more brutal than Will had imagined. He staggered backwards, his shoulder immediately in pain, the fingers of his left hand numb from the shock of the percussion.

'Wow!' he yelled, noticing a furious zinging in his right ear.

'God, that was *loud*!' Jamie's face had gone very pale.

They looked at the smoking gun, then up at the sign, bewildered when they saw no damage at all.

'You loser!' Jamie smirked. 'You only went and missed it.'

'I can't have.' Will was mortified.

'You did. Look.'

'But . . . ' Will reddened with embarrasment.

'No buts, mate. You bloody missed it. I *thought* the barrel went up when you fired it. The bullets went too high.'

'I never missed it. They must be blanks.'

'What?'

'That's the only answer. I know my dad's got blanks. I must have got the wrong box.'

'Nah. You're just a lousy shot.'

'They're blanks!' Will gave him a hard stare.

'No they're not.'

Will ejected the cartridge and put a fresh one in the breach.

'I'm telling you.'

'You can't shoot. That's the problem.'

'I'm one hundred per cent certain they're blanks.' Will swung the barrel round until it pointed at Jamie's thigh. 'Look, I could pull the trigger now and nothing would happen.'

59

ON BOARD BA225, HEATHROW AIRPORT

Ren's flight had not moved an inch. There had been no further update from the captain but it was evident to all on board that there was still no gate available for them to move onto. The Japanese businessman was checking his watch on a minute by minute basis, his anxiety levels steadily rising at the thought of his daughter who he figured must surely be on the summit of Everest by now.

He was starting to feel a little ill with the stress. The air conditioning on the plane seemed to have given up the fight. Droplets of sweat pricked the back of his neck. He had the sensation of breathlessness and an awkward feeling of increasing claustrophobia.

He pressed the call button again, summoning the air hostess.

'How long is it going to be before I can get off this aircraft?' he asked her abruptly.

'I really can't say, sir, but I'm sure it will be soon.'

Ren showed her his mobile. 'This call I'm waiting for. It's from my daughter, you see. She's a climber, she's on Mount Everest and—'

The air hostess cut him short. 'I'm very sorry, sir, but rules are rules. I can't let you use the phone while you're still on board.'

Ren could see by the flinty look in her eyes that he wasn't going to win this argument. He sat back in his seat, restless and irritated as the hostess continued to keep an eye on him. He looked out of the window as other aircraft taxied past them towards the runway, praying for a gate to come free.

60

CHINCHEWE VILLAGE, MALAWI, EAST AFRICA

Tina's husband Martin had just stepped out of the front door of the Africa Frontline Care clinic when a white Toyota Land Cruiser came racing up the drive. The driver skidded to a stop in a cloud of red dust, and a local woman climbed out and rushed towards him, an unconscious child lying limply in her arms.

'Please help my son!' she cried, almost throwing the bloodied infant at Martin in her desperation. 'Please do something for him!'

Martin pulled back the rag which covered the boy's lower body, flinching when he saw the deep laceration in the thigh. At first he thought the boy may have been stabbed, then he took a closer look.

'This looks like a bite mark,' he said.

'It is. He has been attacked by a baboon.' The mother was weeping uncontrollably now.

'Are you sure? I've never heard of such a thing.'

'It is true,' the driver told him. 'I found him by the fields.'

'When did it happen?'

'I'm not certain. He was almost unconscious when I picked him up.'

'This boy has lost a lot of blood. He's very sick,' Martin told them. 'Let's get him into the clinic.'

Martin swept up the steps and led the way along the corridor into a treatment room.

61

TERMINAL ONE, HEATHROW AIRPORT

Airport thief Mick Vines was still at Terminal One, looking for his first victim of the day. From his vantage point at the coffee shop on the first floor he was able to watch as passengers entered the terminal.

The trick was to look for someone with a problem, that was always the key. It didn't matter what the problem was, it could be a mother trying to cope with a child throwing a tantrum, a couple in the throws of a row, a businessman late for his flight, desperately searching for his passport in a coat pocket.

That was when Mick would make his move, striking with total confidence. He never looked over his shoulder or scanned the crowds around to see if someone had spotted him—for that was often the very behaviour which caused a thief to *be* spotted. No, experience had taught him that keeping his head down was the answer, moving casually to the target and lifting the bag as if it was his and he was just returning to reclaim it.

As soon as he had the bag, he would slip it into the large carrier bag which he always carried in his left hand on these jobs. Then it was time to walk away, nerves heightened in case he had been spotted.

Mick took another sip of coffee, watching the busy concourse beneath him. Today felt good, he thought, it had the smell of big money, just a gut feeling that he sometimes had.

62

CHINCHEWE VILLAGE, MALAWI, EAST AFRICA

Martin placed the child on the examination table and pulled on some disposable surgical gloves as his assistant entered the room.

'This bite has severed the femoral artery,' he told the assistant, 'get a torniquet on him while I do a blood type analysis.'

Martin performed the test, finding that the child was blood group A+.

'He's going to need a blood transfusion. Check the fridge for plasma.'

'I don't need to check it,' the assistant told him, 'we used it all last week on that truck driver.'

'Then we need the flying doctor service to fly some up,' Martin told his assistant. 'Can we get on the line to Lilongwe?'

'The phones are still down,' the assistant replied.

Martin cursed beneath his breath; the telephone lines to the capital had been out of action for days.

Martin ran to his office and took the satellite telephone case from the rack. The unit was phenomenally expensive to run at thirty dollars a minute but if there was ever a case that justified an emergency call then this was it.

Martin plugged the module in and adjusted the aerial to the indicated position. Then he dialled the number which would connect him to the flying doctor emergency service in Lilongwe.

63

EVEREST SUMMIT, NEPAL

Kuni knew she could wait no longer. The day was already drawing to a close, the larger peaks casting shadows across the lesser summits of the Himalayas, the glaciers and valleys of Nepal so dark now that she could see no detail in their depths. More troubling, a thick bank of menacing looking clouds had gathered to the south.

Her radio crackled in the breast pocket of her wind suit. 'Kuni. We still can't get any response from your father in the UK. We've been trying non stop but now you really have to get down to top camp.'

Kuni took one last look around the summit, breathing the frosted air deep into her lungs—feeling an intense glow of almost spiritual satisfaction that she had achieved her ambition. But that elation was deadened by the communication problems which had robbed her of her chance to speak to her father in that most important of moments. She felt cheated, as if she had been robbed of something very precious—very personal.

A deep shiver passed through Kuni as a fast moving gust of wind raced across the summit. Just as fast was a sense of something which chilled her even further—the sixth sense that many climbers speak of was ringing an almost inaudible alarm bell deep in her subconscious.

She looked down at the slope beneath her, the sixty degree ice field which was her only exit down to the ridge. Kuni flexed the muscles in her arms and legs, trying to warm herself with some stretching exercises. Then she pressed the transmit button:

'This is Kuni. OK, I'm not going to wait any longer. There's some bad looking clouds coming in. I'm leaving the summit now.'

64

SAUNCY WOOD, WILTSHIRE, UK

BANG! Will recoiled with the blast and then looked with satisfaction at the damage the shot had done to the tree. Small pieces of splintered bark cascaded down around the two boys and there was a gratifyingly big hole of shattered white wood in the mature trunk.

'There you go,' Jamie told him, 'told you they weren't blanks. You just missed that sign back there fair and square. Plus if you'd actually shot the bloody thing at me you would have had my leg off.'

'All right, smartarse.' Will had to concede his friend was right, their tense stand-off back at the road had almost ended with a disaster and it made him shiver to think how close he had actually been to pulling the trigger on his friend.

Luckily, Jamie had persuaded him that they should wander back into the forest and test his blanks theory on a tree instead.

Jamie checked his watch. 'I'm going home now. Which way are the bikes?'

Will gave him a sad look. 'What? You mean you don't know?'

Jamie looked around him. He had to concede he was completely lost. He shrugged as Will smiled.

'Tell you what. I'll guide you to the bikes, *if* you help me go and get that deer.'

'What are you on about now?'

'We'll get a trophy after all. We'll go and get that dead

deer we saw earlier, take it home and skin it so we can show the others the horns.'

'But we didn't shoot it.'

'They don't know that. And we're not going to tell them are we?'

'I just want to go and get my bike.'

'Go on then.' Will gestured into the forest with a smirk, knowing that Jamie could never find the bikes without him. Then he led the way which would take them back towards the bushes where they had found the dying deer, Jamie dragging his heels behind.

65

CHAMPLAIN, WASHINGTON DC, USA

It was now almost seven a.m. in Washington. Shelton Marriner could see the sun rising through the garage window as he put the last of the jerrycans into place in the back of the van.

He went back into the house to retrieve the final piece of the plan, a tin trunk which was hidden in the basement. The temperature down there was intensely hot thanks to the several domestic heaters which Shelton had kept on day and night. Nitroglycerine is much more effective, and more receptive to a detonating charge, when it is warm.

Shelton's army training had taught him that, just as it had taught him how to plan and execute the raid on the local quarry blasting company who had been the rightful owners of the high explosive.

It had all been so easy. So far.

The trunk was an awkward size, and the sixty kilogrammes of high explosive it contained was almost more weight than Shelton could bear. He was sweating abundantly as he reached the van.

The tin trunk slotted nicely into the space between the jerrycans. Shelton opened the trunk lid, letting the sweet marzipan smell of the nitroglycerine fill the cramped compartment. He rolled on some rubber gloves and pulled some components from a bag.

In front of him were two charges, two sections of detonator cord, and sufficient firing cable to reach to the front console of the van. Power would be from the van battery, the initiator switch already built into the front dashboard of the Chevrolet and tested ready for use. Shelton could feel himself becoming a little faint from the nitroglycerine fumes. He poked his head out of the rear of the van to get some fresher air, then picked up the wire cutters and retreated back into the interior.

66

ON BOARD BA225, HEATHROW AIRPORT

Ren Hayashi's flight had been motionless for almost forty minutes before the captain finally announced the gate was free. Then it took a further five minutes for the aircraft to move to the stand where the airbridge was connected. Itching with impatience, Ren was one of the first out of his seat once the seat belt signs were finally turned off.

As soon as he was out of the aircraft door, Ren was switching on his mobile where he found he had three messages waiting for him. He paged the message service as he walked briskly into the terminal.

'Mr Hayashi? This is Tony at base camp, I have some great news for you which is that Kuni is on the summit right now and is in great shape. She's longing to talk to you and we'll keep trying you every few minutes on this number. Alternatively, if you have a problem with this mobile number, call us on a landline, you've got the satphone number.'

The second message was similar, so Ren skipped to the third which was the patched through voice of his daughter herself sounding breathless and strained.

'Dad? Where are you? I'm on the summit of the world and I've been waiting to speak to you! Anyway, don't worry about me, everything's gone fine. I love you, Dad, and I'll speak to you later OK? Sorry we didn't speak while I was here but I really have to get back down now. Call base camp as soon as you can OK?'

Ren's heart sank. So he *had* missed the moment. Tears

pricked at his eyes as he looked round the arrivals hall. Experience of the last few weeks had taught him the connections to Everest were much better from a landline. He wanted to use a payphone.

There. A line of BT payboxes at the far side of the hall.

67

CHINCHEWE VILLAGE, MALAWI, EAST AFRICA

In the back room of the clinic, Martin was still trying to raise Lilongwe on the satellite telephone. Call after call had been logged through, but the flying doctor service was stubbornly engaged. Some time in the next hour Martin knew the Red Cross aeroplane would be taking off for the north.

He *had* to contact them before that flight left Lilongwe, and get them to divert to Chinchewe with the blood plasma for the child.

The problem—common to all satellite phones—was that every time Martin got connected, the satellite system immediately billed for a minute of call time even though he wasn't speaking to anyone. The unit had a daily limit of three hundred dollars and he'd wasted over two hundred getting nowhere at all.

He thought through his options, deciding that he would try and relay a call through the British Embassy in the capital. He dialled the number but the line was extremely weak.

'Hello, this is Martin Curtis at the Africa Frontline Care clinic up at Chinchewe. Can you put me through to the first secretary please?'

'He is at a conference all day, I'm afraid.'

'Then the information office.'

'I can't hear you, caller. Can you call back on a better line please?' The call was cut.

'Damn.' Martin was running out of call time. Then he thought of Tina. His wife would be perfect; Martin knew she would understand the situation immediately and act fast. Martin checked his watch, trying to recall what flight his wife was taking that day. If he could only get hold of her before she flew . . .

Martin dialled the international code for England, punching in the numbers for Tina's mobile and hoping, for the child's sake, that he was going to find her.

68

TERMINAL ONE, HEATHROW AIRPORT

Mick spotted his target, a distinguished looking Japanese businessman in his mid fifties. He was striding at some speed across the terminal, heading for a payphone. It was hard to assess what attracted him to the target, other than the fact that the Japanese businessman seemed agitated and somewhat overheated.

He had a briefcase and an overnight case on wheels—another little plus point for Mick as two bags are always harder for a target to handle than one. He looked as if he was worth money too; Mick reckoned his suit was a five hundred pound job at least. There were no large bulges in the suit pockets—chances were high that the target's wallet would be in the briefcase. Even at this distance, Mick could see there was a sheen of sweat coating the target's brow—this Japanese guy was seriously stressed out.

Mick paid for his coffee and slipped on his coat. It was time to take a closer look.

69

TERMINAL ONE, HEATHROW AIRPORT

Tina had parked her Audi in the staff car park and was walking towards the administration block in Terminal One when her mobile rang.

'Hello.'

'Tina?' On a crackly line she heard her husband calling from Africa.

'Tina?'

'Hi, darling, this is a nice surprise!'

'Thank God I got you. Where are you?'

'I'm at Heathrow. God, I've had a hell of a morning, Martin, it's been a right . . .'

But Martin cut her off.

'Listen, I need your help. We've got a bloody nightmare here.'

Tina was picking up the clipped tone of her husband, realizing quickly that something was wrong with his voice.

'Are you all right?'

'I'm OK, but we've got a serious problem here with a patient and all the landlines are down from here to Lilongwe. This satellite phone is my only means of communication, and you're my best chance to get a message through.'

'OK. What do you need me to do?'

70

TERMINAL ONE, HEATHROW AIRPORT

Ren crossed hastily to the nearest telephone and pushed a handful of pound coins into the slot. He placed his two bags on the floor by his feet, took out his diary to refer to the number, then dialled the Inmarsat number of the expedition satellite receiver in Nepal, biting his lip nervously as he waited.

'Base camp.'

'This is Ren.'

'Hey, we've been trying to get you for the last hour. Did you get the message Kuni reached the summit?'

'I did. I'm very happy about that. Can you put me through to her?'

'Well, she's on the descent now but I'll radio her right away and let's see if we can get her. Hold on to the line.'

'No problem.'

71

TERMINAL ONE, HEATHROW AIRPORT

Mick Vines walked down the stairway and joined the busy throng of travellers on the terminal concourse. He was keeping a sharp eye on the Japanese businessman, flashing a glance in his direction every few seconds to check exactly what he had done with his bags.

The precise position of the bags was crucial. Mick would not be able to carry out the heist if they were resting against the target's leg.

He stopped by a departures board, scanning the listed flights with an anxious air, then flashed a look at his watch.

Now he just needed the Japanese man to turn his line of sight away from the concourse so the bags were behind him. He could see that the man was still distracted. In fact it looked as if he was having problems with his connection which was all good news for Mick.

The thief was poised. Ready to act. All it needed was for the Japanese man to angle his body a little more towards the wall and the job was on.

72

EVEREST NORTH FACE, NEPAL

Kuni was into the descent, moving as fast as she could down the steep ice field when her radio went off in her pocket.

'Kuni, this is base camp. Base camp, over.'

Her first reaction was to ignore it, she was on extremely exposed ground and she knew that the slope had avalanched in the past with catastrophic results. Worse still, she could see a narrow crack had opened up in the face, a grey shadow of fractured ice which snaked almost fifty metres across the summit pyramid. Kuni knew it was a potentially lethal sign, that the snowpack had shifted, a clear cut indication that the face was definitely not stable.

But the radio blurted out again and through the rising wind Kuni thought she heard the words 'your father'. She came to a halt, pushing her ice axe deep into the snow to act as a support, then took the radio out of her pocket.

'This is Kuni.'

'We've got your father on the line! Wait just a moment.'

73

TERMINAL ONE, HEATHROW AIRPORT

'I need you to call Innocent Mwanza at the clinic in the capital,' Martin told Tina. 'Tell him I have a critically injured eight-year-old boy here at the lake clinic. He's been bitten by a baboon. I need the flying doctor service to fly up urgently with at least six sachets of blood plasma. Type A+.'

Martin gave her the number and international code for the flying doctor service.

'I'll call them right away,' Tina told him.

'Great. Keep trying until you get them. It's the only chance this boy has got.'

Suddenly, the line went dead.

'Hello? Martin?'

Tina looked for a payphone to make the international call to the Malawian capital. To her left were two BT telephones, one occupied by a Japanese man, the other free. Tina crossed to it and dialled the number Martin had given her, finding to her frustration that it was engaged. She called once more, then again, but the result was the same.

She checked her watch; time was slipping by. She really should be checking in to the operations centre in the next two or three minutes.

74

SIX LAKES THEME PARK, NEAR WINDSOR, UK

Sophie clutched tightly at her father's hand as the Junior Dragon roller coaster moved slowly up the track, the metal teeth of the wagons clanking as they bit into the rack.

This was the smallest roller coaster in the park, far inferior to the brutal looking Tormentor which loomed to their right, but the incline was still thrillingly steep for the young girl, the delicious sense of anticipation increasing with every second as the cars kept climbing towards the high point where the real thrills would begin.

'How you feeling, love?' Dean asked her.

'I can't look!' Sophie slammed her hand over her eyes as the park fell away beneath them. Then she sneaked a peek, giggling uncontrollably with nerves as she saw that they were higher than most of the buildings.

The wagons reached the top of the incline. They paused there for a second or two, creeping forward on the crest with smoking cauldrons beneath them.

Then they were off, the buggy shooting down the rails as Sophie let out a manic scream of delight.

75

EVEREST NORTH FACE, NEPAL

Kuni slipped off her rucksack, turned and dropped back into the snow to sit while she took the call.

'Kuni? It's me.'

As her body hit the slope, the tiny shock wave travelled across the ice face. The critical layers of ice adhesion were poised on a hair-trigger and the impact of her body was enough to set an avalanche in motion. It happened so fast that Kuni's feet were swept away in an instant, her body immediately sliding down the steep angled slope, the top slab of ice crust breaking up and tumbling around her as she fell heavily onto her flank.

She snatched at her ice axe, her fingers just missing the vital tool as she began to accelerate down the slope.

Within seconds she was spinning out of control, her arms flailing, her hands desperately clawing at the face as she tried to arrest her fall. The slope began to disintegrate around her, the ice blocks turning to powder which billowed up in a wall like the crest of a breaking wave. Kuni found herself in a white turmoil of snow, her lungs filling with freezing powder even as she screamed.

76

TERMINAL ONE, HEATHROW AIRPORT

Tina was on her fifth attempt to get through to Malawi when something strange caught her attention. If she hadn't turned her head suddenly to glance at her watch, she never would have seen it.

A man in a dark overcoat had walked past the payphone where the Japanese businessman next to her was engrossed in a conversation. As he did so, the man in the overcoat stooped slightly to pick up one of the bags which had been placed on the floor behind the Japanese guy's feet. It was expertly done, Tina had to concede, in fact so expertly done that for a moment the pilot was inclined to believe the bag actually belonged to the man in the dark overcoat.

But then she saw the bag disappear into a larger plastic shopping bag as the perpetrator walked confidently away. That was certainly odd. Why would the guy in the overcoat slip that bag into another bag? And why so fast? Tina tapped the Japanese man on the shoulder.

'Have you lost one of your bags?' she asked him.

The Japanese businessman looked at her, startled, then looked behind him.'Yes! Did you see someone take it?'

'I did. In fact I can see him now.'

'Which one?'

'The dark overcoat.'

'Hey!' Ren called after the thief. 'Hey, you!'

77

EVEREST NORTH FACE, NEPAL

Kuni felt the world drop away, a heartbeat of total terror as she imagined the avalanche would sweep her right off the face of Everest. Then the crushing impact of bone against ice and she came to a dead halt. Ice blocks piled in on top of her, tons of the stuff, until her lungs were struggling to get air. A dull but nevertheless serious pain began to speak of trauma to her right thigh.

All was quiet. The avalanche was over. But where the hell was she and how had she survived?

Kuni pushed powder snow away from her face, creating a small air pocket in which to breathe. She flexed her arms, finding that she could lever herself up against the heavy block of ice which was pinning her down.

The block shifted. Daylight filtered through the snow.

She was lying at the bottom of a crevasse, a steep-sided fissure cut into the mountain ice.

Kuni gasped for breath as the pain in her thigh suddenly raged harder.

78

TERMINAL ONE, HEATHROW AIRPORT

Calder Lawton was browsing through the racks at the Terminal One music store searching for the new CD by Coldplay while he waited for his Moscow flight to be called. One of the Russian technicians at Space City—a serious fan of the band—had asked the American astronaut to bring him a copy of the album and Calder was using this brief London stopover to keep his promise.

He had just found the CD when he heard a shout out in the main concourse. At the same moment a man in a dark overcoat walked very quickly past the shop entrance. He caught Calder's attention because he was moving so fast.

'Stop that man,' a Japanese man was calling, 'he's got my bag.'

Calder moved out of the shop onto the concourse, trying to keep the overcoat man in sight. The terminal was crowded but Calder could see the top of overcoat man's head, moving through the dense crowds of passengers. He was striding quickly towards the exit and would soon be out of the building. Calder began to run after him, fighting his way through a tightly packed group of elderly travellers who were queuing for a check in.

'Hey!' he called. 'Stop that guy!'

79

EVEREST NORTH FACE, NEPAL

Kuni scrabbled with her hands, pushing smaller chunks of ice away from her as she enlarged the hole. The pain in her thigh began to escalate even more as she tried to extricate her leg. She twisted her body, pulling ahead with both hands, finally feeling the pressure lift as she rolled onto some iceblocks and found herself free.

She lay on her side, traumatized and in shock, her mind—already dulled by the enervating effects of high altitude and the rigours of her climb to Everest's summit—was struggling to come to terms with this abrupt and potentially fatal turn of events.

The slope had avalanched. Just beneath the summit.

Kuni recalled that her last action had been to sit backwards into the snow—and she now realized that the seemingly innocent force involved had unleashed the avalanche that had swept her away. She craned her neck, looking up and trying to make sense of her situation.

And wondering if she could escape the trap.

80

TERMINAL ONE, HEATHROW AIRPORT

The astronaut continued to thread his way through the crowds, desperately trying to keep the thief's head in view. But the robber had a twenty metre headstart and Calder's cries had alerted him. Now, he too was moving almost at a run, closing quickly on the revolving door which led out to the covered loading rank outside the terminal.

Calder could see that the loading area was thick with passengers queuing for taxis and buses; if the thief got into that melee he could easily melt away.

'Someone stop that man! The guy in the dark coat!' he called out, getting a few shocked looks from other members of the public, all of whom were too embarrassed—or uncertain—to take action. Still the thief was moving towards the door.

Calder could see fast movement to his right, noticing with relief that a uniformed policeman had responded to his cries and was running towards the action. Now Calder and the cop were side by side, running at full tilt towards the exit as the thief ran from the terminal into the busy crowds outside.

81

SIX LAKES THEME PARK, NEAR WINDSOR, UK

'Yaaaaey!' Sophie shrieked as the roller coaster shot down the steepest section of the ride, picking up impressive speed in just two or three seconds, then sending their stomachs skyward as it spiralled and lurched into a banking turn. They gained momentum as the cars zoomed across the moat, Sophie's nails digging into Dean's hand as they sped past Shelley, madly waving from the barrier.

'There's your mum!' Dean yelled as he pointed out the tiny figure flashing past them. 'Give her a wave.'

Sophie took her hand off the safety bar for a brief moment to do it, then wrapped her fingers back round it, her knuckles white and scrunched up as they went into the next turn.

'Smile for the camera!' Dean told his daughter as he saw the photo sign racing towards them. Sophie managed a manic smile, her eyes watering with the speed of the wind on her face.

Kaboom! The battery of flashlights fired off in their faces and then they were entering the tunnel where the luminous outlines of phantoms and dragons shot past at breakneck speed.

82

TERMINAL ONE, HEATHROW AIRPORT

Mick was five paces from the door, with the two pursuers now right at his heels. He reached the doorway, smashing into an Asian couple, sending their bags flying off their trolley as they sprawled backwards to the floor. Mick jumped over them, hit the loading bay area, and took his sharp right turn. But the black American guy was too fast for him, and the cop wasn't far behind.

Mick half turned as he sensed the American was one step behind him. The tackle caught him on the side of his body, throwing him violently to the floor and sending the bag spinning across the pavement towards the road.

Mick hit the ground hard, the wind knocked momentarily out of his body as the have-a-go hero and the cop both grabbed at his coat.

It seemed as if it was all over but the thief had one last line of defence and now he was going to use it.

83

EVEREST NORTH FACE, NEPAL

One thing was instantly clear to Kuni as she looked around the crevasse—there was no easy way out. Kuni had seen crevasses where one end tapers out into a snow ramp offering an easy walk to safety. But this one had steep walls on all sides, not so steep that they couldn't be climbed, but steep enough to offer a serious climbing challenge even to a fit climber at sea level. Kuni knew she was injured—her thigh was throbbing now with much more than the pain of a mere bruise. She didn't want to look at the damage. Not yet.

The radio. Kuni knew she had to alert base camp to her predicament.

The Japanese climber realized she still had the walkie-talkie in her hand. At least she had not lost that vital lifeline. Maybe her father was still on the line? Her frozen fingers fumbled with the tiny controls.

'Dad? Can you hear me? Are you there?'

There was no reply.

'Dad! This is Kuni, can you hear me?'

84

TERMINAL ONE, HEATHROW AIRPORT

In the inside pocket of his overcoat Mick Vines kept a cannister of mace—a souvenir from a trip to Florida, smuggled back into the UK for just such an emergency.

The CN gas the cannister contained was designed for use by victims of crime—a foolproof deterrent for use against rapists or muggers, and equally effective in the situation Mick was now trying to escape from.

As his two pursuers tightened their grips, Mick managed to get his hand into the pocket. He found the cannister, flipping off the top with his thumb and firing off the aerosol of CN gas right into the faces of his attackers.

85

SIX LAKES THEME PARK, NEAR WINDSOR, UK

The roller coaster crabbed round the final bend and began to slow. A few heartbeats later Sophie and Dean were braking to a halt and the lap bars were released with a pneumatic hiss.

'Again!' Sophie's eyes were shining with the thrill of the ride. 'One more time, Dad, go on!'

'Not now, princess, I'll buy you the photo and we'll go and find another ride.'

Dean consulted his map of the park. 'I'll tell you what, why don't we go panning for gold on the Crazy Nuggets, see if you can find some treasure.'

Dean bought Sophie the picture of the two of them on the Junior Dragon and the family made their way through the park towards the treasure hunt stand.

'Don't let me forget the twelve thirty race,' Dean told Shelley as they went, 'I've got my radio with me.'

'What are you talking about?'

'The race. Sophie's Day at Newbury. Wouldn't want to miss it, would we?'

86

TERMINAL ONE, HEATHROW AIRPORT

Tina had watched the Japanese businessman rush off through the terminal in pursuit of his bag. Now she noticed that he had left the telephone receiver hanging on its cord. She put the receiver to her ear and thought she could hear the voice of a Japanese girl, very faint and distorted, coming down the line.

'Hello? Can you speak English?' Tina asked the Japanese voice, wanting to explain why the caller had suddenly rushed away. There was a confused silence from the other end, accompanied by a great deal of static interference, then Tina thought she could hear English words being spoken.

'Can you speak louder?' she said into the handset. 'I can hardly hear you.'

87

TERMINAL ONE, HEATHROW AIRPORT

Calder let out a scream as the mace hit home, getting the full impact of the anti-mugger spray full in the face at point-blank range. The cop was a little luckier, he was able to turn his head away as he saw the cannister raised to fire, but Calder got it right in the eyes from a distance of about six inches or so.

The pain was instant and all consuming, the effect exactly as if someone had flung a cannister of acid right into the soft tissue of his eyeballs.

Calder let go of the bag thief, bringing his hands up to his face in a reflex action, as he screwed up his face and let out a shouted curse. Then the tear gas was in his lungs, the spray causing a shock of temporary paralysis and actually stopping his breathing for a second or two. He began to choke, falling onto his side as he sensed people reaching for him.

88

EVEREST NORTH FACE, NEPAL

Kuni looked at the walkie-talkie in utter confusion. Then she noticed the battery alert was flashing. In a few seconds it would die completely.

'I have to speak to my father. I've been caught in an avalanche, I'm stuck in a crevasse. Tell him to call base camp . . .'

With a terminal click the walkie-talkie died. Kuni took a look at the LCD display. The batteries were totally dead. Now she was in a trap and with no way of alerting base camp.

Kuni looked around her, realizing that this would probably be the place where she would die.

89

TERMINAL ONE, HEATHROW AIRPORT

'Are you all right, sir?' A young policewoman arrived at Calder's side while her colleagues dealt with the bag thief.

'You gotta get me to a bathroom fast,' he told the policewoman, 'I need to get some water, rinse this stuff out of my eyes.'

She took him by the arm and ushered him quickly back into the terminal, taking him to the nearest washroom. Calder got his head beneath a tap and let the cool water sluice across his eyes, forcing them open in the attempt to relieve the excruciating pain of the mace.

'We need to get you to the first aid room,' the policewoman told him, 'come with me.'

90

TERMINAL ONE, HEATHROW AIRPORT

Ren burst out of the terminal just in time to see five or six burly policemen restraining the thief on the forecourt floor. One had the thief's arm behind his back, while another brought out a set of plasticuffs to immobilize him. There was an acrid smell of gas in the air, and Hayashi felt his eyes begin to water.

Hayashi was dismayed to see that his bag had burst open in the drama, his laptop, personal organizer, and wallet lying on the concrete floor. He crouched down to gather the objects back together, then watched for a few seconds as the police continued their struggle, wondering if he should stay to give them a statement.

But no one was paying him any attention, and the realization that his daughter may still be on the telephone was a more pressing concern. Ren slipped away, rushing back into the terminal towards the telephone, hoping against hope that his daughter would still be on the line. When he got back to the telephone he was grateful to find that the female pilot was still there, guarding his other overnight case. But to his dismay the phone was back on the hook.

'Did they get him?' she asked.

'Yes, they got him, but what about the telephone? I was speaking to my daughter. Did you hang the phone up?'

'I took the liberty of trying to speak to the person you were calling,' Tina explained, suddenly embarrassed, 'but it was a little difficult to hear.'

'I'm not surprised, she's on Mount Everest.'

'Mount Everest? Well that would explain what I thought I heard.'

'What did you hear? Tell me, please.'

91

FIELDS ABOVE CHINCHEWE VILLAGE, MALAWI, EAST AFRICA

The baboons had seized their opportunity after the injured Kamuzu had left the field, ripping down plants and tearing off the cobs with their teeth. The cobs were dessicated but still sweet, giving the creatures the sugar they craved above all else and firing their bellies with the desire for more. They fought over possession of the juicier kernels; bad-tempered, brutal battles accompanied by snarling threats and wide, staring eyes.

Then they had retreated back into the safety of the forest, resting for a while in the hottest hour of the day. The baboons had eaten well, better than any time in the recent, hungry weeks—but the meal had far from satisfied them. They needed more, but could they risk a further raid back into the field? They had chased away the injured boy but there might now be a dog to contend with—or a strong villager with a gun.

But the skirmish with the child had left the pack in a confident mood—man no longer seemed the foe he had once been. For too long the baboons had feared the human guardians with their sticks and whips. Now, following the lead of the alpha male, they were prepared for a further battle.

The alpha male was watching the field closely. On a small platform another guardian had appeared, and the baboons could see immediately that it was another child—perhaps even smaller than the one they had just beaten off his land.

The thought of all that corn made the risk worthwhile. The alpha male gave a series of rallying cries, the pack responding with their own encouraging barks. Then they became silent, following their leader down through the scrubby vegetation along a dry water course, making their way cautiously back towards the field.

92

TERMINAL ONE, HEATHROW AIRPORT

Tina thought back to the few scrambled words she had picked out amid the distortion and wind rush of the call: 'I thought I heard her say the words, "avalanche, crevasse",' she told Ren.

Ren frowned, wondering at the significance of the words, then he thanked Tina for her help and picked up the telephone once again, to re-establish contact with base camp.

He dialled frantically, finally getting through on the fourth attempt.

'Hello, Tony. This is Ren in London.'

'Oh . . . er . . . Ren did you manage to speak to Kuni when you were connected to her just now?'

Ren thought Tony sounded strained and unnatural.

'Not exactly, why?'

There was a long pause at the other end of the line. Ren could feel his throat go dry with fear.

'Because I'm afraid we may have some extremely bad news for you. One of the team was watching her through binoculars and it seems that just about the time you were connected to her an avalanche swept down the face. Right where your daughter was standing.'

'Oh my God.' Ren felt the world closing in on him in the most malevolent way.

'Now we can't see her. And her radio is out of action.'

Ren gulped in mouthfuls of air as he tried to hold it together. He was already suffering from the effects of inhaling the tear gas, breathless and hyper after the chase to retrieve his stolen bag. And now . . . what was he to make of this devastating news from base camp?

Could his daughter really be dead?

93

CHAMPLAIN, DISTRICT OF COLUMBIA, USA

Shelton Marriner drove down the dirt trail from his farmhouse and turned onto the road which would lead him towards the 95 Interstate. The traffic was light at this hour of the morning, just the earliest commuters and construction workers out and about. The day was going to be a hot one, the air heavy and humid. Shelton could feel prickles of sweat gathering under his arms and at the back of his neck. He kept on the Interstate to the edge of the city, then, not wanting to risk getting pulled over at a toll booth, turned off onto one of the quieter state roads to continue his journey. As he drove he wondered if he could risk a stop to pick up a coffee and a pastry.

A last breakfast. He liked the thought.

Why the hell not? It wasn't in the plan but he was hungry enough. He stopped at a drive-in deli, making sure he chose one where he could keep the van in his line of sight while he paid for the breakfast.

Back in his van, Shelton took a sip of coffee, wincing as the over-hot liquid scalded his lips. *Why the hell don't those people learn?* he asked himself, the anger boiling up instantly—*How difficult is it to make a goddam coffee that doesn't scald?*

He was tempted to go back and throw the contents of the cup in the attendant's face. But then he saw the photograph of his two boys on the dashboard and reminded himself that more important things were at hand.

He put the coffee in the cup-holder and turned onto the National route, keeping to the speed limit and tuning into the local FM station to check the traffic reports as he made his way into the city.

94

TERMINAL ONE, HEATHROW AIRPORT

Ren's mind was racing, thinking back to the conversation with the pilot. Avalanche had been one of the words the pilot thought she had heard, and the other . . . ?

'Crevasse,' Ren told Tony, 'I think she's in a crevasse, that was the last word she used on the radio. Is that possible?'

'Listen, Mr Hayashi, it's extremely unlikely. Even if she *was* somehow swept into a crevasse, the chances that she would survive would be very thin.'

'Yes, but there's always a chance, right?'

'Well, maybe . . .'

A sudden vision flashed into Ren's mind; a horrific photograph of a dead climber he had seen in an Everest book, a frozen corpse which would never be retrieved. The thought that this might be Kuni's fate was too much to contemplate.

'No maybe, she *has* to be in a crevasse, Tony, that was the word she used. You've got to send someone up to look for her, she needs rescue.'

'It's not so simple as that, Ren,' Tony snapped, 'our nearest climbers are at camp five and that's a thousand metres lower than her position.'

'You've got to find someone to rescue her,' Ren pleaded, 'she's still alive, I know it.'

'We'll do what we can, Mr Hayashi, there were two German climbers on the summit at the same time as Kuni. I'll see if we can contact them.'

'Do that. Do anything you can! And call me back on the

mobile as soon as you have news.' Ren put down the phone and crossed to a nearby sales desk.

'Can you get me a flight to Kathmandu?' he demanded. 'It's most urgent.'

95

TERMINAL ONE, HEATHROW AIRPORT

The cloud of tear gas had taken a while to clear, but as soon as the police officers could breathe again, Mick Vines was dragged to his feet and bundled towards a waiting riot van.

He was thrown none too gently into the back and two burly officers got in to guard him.

'I am arresting you for theft, common assault, and possession of an illegal weapon,' the commanding officer told him. 'You do not have to say anything, but it may harm your defence if you do not mention when questioned something which you later rely on in court. Anything you do say may be given in evidence.'

'Whatever,' Mick spat back.

Mick rubbed at his eyes and cursed his luck. To be done for theft was one thing, but using the mace had been his big mistake. Tear gas was a banned substance and using it at an airport could even be seen as an act of terrorism.

Mick had previous. He had been up before the courts before but on those occasions he had been convicted of straightforward theft and got away lightly with a couple of months in open jails where the regime was scarcely rigorous enough to be considered a punishment.

He knew this time would be different. A lengthy custodial sentence in a hell-hole like Wormwood Scrubs or Pentonville was inevitable. He tried to guess how long it would be before he tasted freedom again. It could easily be three years. Perhaps even five. Long enough for his wife and two increasingly troublesome teenage sons to write him out of their lives entirely.

What a mess, Mick thought, how could he have got things so wrong? The commanding officer snapped an order to the driver and the van pulled away towards London.

96

TERMINAL ONE, HEATHROW AIRPORT

Tina made her way to the flight crew logistics area, putting her baggage through the X-ray security device and showing her security pass to gain access to the controlled zone.

Airside now, she walked the corridor to the programming room where flight operations director Ross Hawker and his colleagues were busy juggling with the logistical problems of the day.

'Hi, Ross,' she told him, 'so sorry I was delayed getting in.'

'Don't worry. At least you *made* it in, unlike the staff who've called in sick today.'

The duty manager burrowed into his information source on the screen. 'Oh yes. Seattle, wasn't it?'

'That's right.'

'I've had to allocate it for another crew.'

'What have you given me?'

'The Four Nine Two. Moscow.'

'Who's the co-pilot?'

'Graham Ravenscroft.'

'Overnight?'

'No. It's an out and about. Oh, and you'd better get straight off to stand forty-two, we've already had to cancel three earlier flights because of staff shortages.'

'On my way,' Tina told him, then she paused as she saw the look of concern that flashed across Ross's face.

'Are you sure you're all right?' he asked. 'You look . . . I don't know . . . stressed out or something.'

'No, I'm fine,' Tina told him, but there was no hiding the way her voice faltered. Hawker handed Tina the dossier containing weather information and route instructions for the Moscow sector.

'Have a good flight.'

97

THE NORTH FACE OF EVEREST, NEPAL

Kuni put the radio carefully back in her pocket, and turned herself into a position where she could look upwards towards the mouth of the crevasse. The lip of the fissure seemed a long way up—perhaps ten metres or more, and the walls were sheer blue ice—the type which would not allow a good purchase for the points of her ice axe and crampons.

With a sudden shock she realized the ice axe was missing. Without it, she was lost. Kuni knew that she had been holding the axe as the slope had avalanched, and that the short length of securing sling had been wrapped around her wrist. Somehow, during the tumbling nightmare of the avalanche the sling had become detached, and Kuni could only assume that the ice axe was buried somewhere in the debris which surrounded her. The rucksack must be in there somewhere too, she thought, but finding it was less of a priority.

Still lying on her side, not wanting to put any weight on her damaged leg, Kuni inched forward and began to scrabble amongst the many hundreds of blocks of ice. The activity brought warm blood flowing to her frozen finger tips, causing her agonizing pain. She gritted her teeth, knowing that she would need the feeling in her fingers to stand any chance of climbing out.

She concentrated on the area near to where she had fallen, scooping the broken blocks of ice away one by one until, finally, her gloved fingers closed around metal. She pulled out the ice axe, a small glow of satisfaction giving her a moment of optimism.

Now at least she could climb.

Or could she? It was time to check out the damage to her leg.

98

TERMINAL ONE, HEATHROW AIRPORT

Calder was in the medical room at Terminal One, having his eyes irrigated by a staff nurse. The process was not exactly a pleasant one, with the top and bottom eyelids pulled right out to enable a fine tube to be inserted through which a sterilized eyewash was fed at some pressure. As the liquid sluiced against his eyes, Calder squinted at the clock on the wall, just able to make out the time with his fuzzy vision.

'I really have to go now,' he told the policewoman, 'my flight will be boarding soon.'

'We need a statement, sir. We can't prosecute without one. Now, what flight are you on?'

'BA to Moscow. Midday.'

'Give me your ticket. I'll go and check if there's another Moscow flight later,' the policewoman told him.

'I have meetings there this afternoon,' Calder told her, 'I really don't want to let those people down.'

'I appreciate that, sir, but you have been the victim of a serious assault. I'm sure you wouldn't want the gentleman to be released without charge would you?'

Calder sat back in his chair. Gentleman, he thought, amazed at the use of the word; only the British could refer to a vicious criminal as a 'gentleman'. 'OK. But you must get me on the very next flight.'

The medical treatment continued and the policewoman came back into the room a few minutes later. 'There's a Jetlink Alliance direct flight to Moscow half an hour later.

I took the liberty of checking it and there are standby seats available.'

'All right,' Calder reluctantly agreed. 'If you can sort it out, I'll do the statement and take that flight. But let's make it fast.'

99

THE NORTH FACE OF EVEREST, NEPAL

Kuni shuffled onto her behind and began to undo the buckles that held the salopette onto her plastic climbing boot. Disturbing her wounded leg was the last thing she wanted to do, but before she could contemplate the climb, she knew she had to check out the damage and stop the bleeding as best she could.

How bad was it? She had to know.

So, with her back to the crevasse wall, she carefully peeled back the Gore-tex gaiters and revealed the blood-soaked windproof material beneath. The down suit had a zip right up each leg, and, with trembling fingers, Kuni now unzipped the fabric.

What she saw made her gasp in astonishment: the broken leg was far, far worse than she had thought—the avalanche had left her with a compound fracture—the femur completely snapped at the midway point with the broken end jutting through an ugly eruption of bloodied flesh.

It was the type of injury that climbers fear most; an injury that is far too grave to be treated on the slopes of a mountain with a first aid kit, the type of trauma that needs surgery in a hospital as a matter of urgency. Then, as if the wound had been waiting for her visual inspection, the pain suddenly kicked in as the natural trauma-related painkillers in her system subsided. Kuni let out a cry of agony, throwing her head back as she howled.

Kuni let the spasm pass, then zipped her wind suit back

over the wounded leg. There was no point in waiting. She was already shivering with the onset of hypothermia. She knew instinctively that if she did not move straight away, then she would probably succumb to the temptation to curl up and die.

She grabbed hold of the ice axe and began to crawl towards the sheer wall of ice.

100

TERMINAL ONE, HEATHROW AIRPORT

Tina made her way through the terminal, passing the duty-free shops and heading for departure gate forty-two. The events of the morning were running through her mind, the incident with the deer still troubling her; she wished there had been time to tell Martin about it when he had called earlier.

She reached the gate, greeted the check-in staff who were waiting there, and was about to enter the walkway to the aircraft when she suddenly remembered.

Martin. The call to Malawi. Tina realized with a spasm of guilt that she had forgotten about his request.

She turned around, walked back across the waiting area to find a payphone. She put in some coins, dialled the number, cursed as it registered engaged yet again. For the next few minutes she dialled continuously, aware that she should really be on board and doing the pre-flights. One of the flight attendants walked over.

'Message from the co-pilot,' she told Tina, 'we can't get our air traffic slot until you're on board.'

'I know that.' Tina managed a thin smile. 'Just give me another moment will you?' She punched the numbers, and gave a sigh of relief as she heard the ringing tone on the line.

Contact. At the very last chance.

Tina relayed the message to the operator at the Lilongwe clinic and learned that the Red Cross flight had not yet left for the north. Having explained the nature of the emergency, Tina received an immediate assurance that the blood plasma would be flown up to the Chinchewe clinic as requested.

Now back to business. She really had to board that flight.

101

THE NORTH FACE OF MOUNT EVEREST, NEPAL

Josef Theilart and Bernard Karl were into their descent, five hundred feet below the summit, negotiating the tricky ridge traverse towards the top of the second step when they got the radio call.

'This is Tony, from the Japanese support team at base camp. Did you see the avalanche?'

'Yeah, we saw it,' Josef replied. 'It looked pretty horrific.'

'We think that Kuni might have been caught.'

'The Japanese girl?'

Josef and Bernard looked back towards the summit pyramid, stunned by this piece of news.

'Yes, and we have reason to think she might still be alive.'

'I don't think so,' Josef told him, 'that slope only goes to one place and that's a fall right down the face.'

'She was on the radio, it seems she might have been swept into a crevasse.'

'A crevasse? Well, the face is vast. There's hundreds of crevasses.'

'Is there any way you could go back up and take a look for her?'

The two German climbers looked at each other. They were already exhausted by their own summit climb and the prospect of going back up was a horrifying one. But they knew they were the only team in the vicinity; apart from Kuni on the summit they had seen no other climbers all day.

'Stand by. Give us some time to think,' Josef told Tony.

The two men slumped back onto the ice, talking wearily through their options as the wind swept the face around them.

102

SAUNCY WOOD, WILTSHIRE, ENGLAND

Will could smell the dead animal before he could see it, the cloying stench of decomposition already filling the air. He crawled into the bushes and took hold of a hoof, a swarm of ugly fat blowflies erupting from the belly of the deer as he dragged it out of the rhododendrons to where Jamie stood with his fingers pinched on his nose.

'Gross out!' Jamie exclaimed, an expression of pure disgust on his face. 'I don't know how the hell you can even touch that thing.'

'Look at its belly,' Will told him with relish, 'you can see all the guts and stuff. Plus those flies have all been laying little yellow eggs in there. Look!'

Jamie turned abruptly away, retching into a bush.

'I told you you're a wimp,' Will said. 'Come on and give me a hand.'

Will took hold of one of the deer's hooves and gestured for Jamie to do the same.

'If you're so desperate for the horns,' Jamie pointed out, 'why don't you just cut off its head?'

'Cos I haven't got a knife, you idiot. Now grab hold of one of these hooves and give me a hand. It's dead, it won't bloody bite you.'

'Let's just leave it.'

'Take it.'

Jamie reluctantly obeyed him, averting his eyes from the horrible wound in the deer's flank, and closing his fingers around the spooky fibrous tissue of the cold hoof.

The two boys began to drag the dead animal through the undergrowth, the cloud of flies following on.

103

SIX LAKES THEME PARK, NEAR WINDSOR, UK

Dean and his family had finished panning for gold and, thoroughly soaked by the experience, were wandering through the park searching for a restaurant when Sophie spotted a balloon seller.

'Can I have one of those, Dad? A fairy! No, a dolphin!'

Dean took a good look at the huge bunch of balloons, helium filled foil monstrosities, some almost bigger than Sophie was.

'We'll get you one later, love, just before we go home.' Dean gave Shelley a wink; he knew the chances were that Sophie would forget about it.

'Just one, Dad! All the other kids have got one!'

'No they haven't.'

'Well most of them have.'

Dean needed a distraction. He pointed across to the Tormentor, the biggest roller coaster in the park, big brother to the one they had already done. 'Look, here's the plan. We'll have lunch, then we'll have a go at the big one. OK?'

'Do you think I'm tall enough?'

'Course you are! No problem, you're just about the tallest girl in your class.'

Sophie was happy with that and a couple of minutes later they were inside the food hall. Shelley went to queue for the burgers as Dean took Sophie to find a place to sit. Finding a vacant table, he checked his watch and brought out his portable radio. He tuned it to Radio Five just as the race commentator announced the runners for the twelve thirty at Newbury.

'What you listening to, Dad?'

'Gee-gees.'

104

ON BOARD FLIGHT 492 TO MOSCOW

Tina hurried down the walkway to the aircraft where she greeted co-pilot Graham Ravenscroft with a handshake. 'I'm so sorry I'm late,' Tina told him, taking the Captain's seat while she turned off her mobile, 'it really has been one of those mornings.'

'You're not the only one,' the co-pilot told her. 'I had the journey from hell myself. The Heathrow express was down and I had to take the bloody tube.'

'How are we looking for a slot?'

'Well we did have provisional at twelve thirty. But they wouldn't confirm until we were two up. I'll put in another request.'

The co-pilot made contact with the control tower, grimacing as he got the news.

'Twelve fifty,' he told her.

'Damn.'

Tina knew that making the call to Malawi had made them miss the slot; if she'd been in the cockpit a few minutes earlier they could have saved twenty minutes on the take-off time. Still, it had been worth it to help her husband out—and if it saved the life of a young child then she was happy.

'Let's get to work.' Tina took the Moscow flight dossier out of her flight bag and the two pilots began their pre-flight checks.

Tina signed the load sheet and the despatch officer left

the cockpit. As he did so the chief cabin steward called in and told her, 'We have one no-show, Captain, a standby pax name of Lawton.'

'We lost our slot,' Tina replied, 'you can give him a couple more minutes.'

105

THE NORTH FACE OF MOUNT EVEREST, NEPAL

The two German climbers rested for a while, drinking from their insulated flasks and sharing a high energy food bar as they thought it through.

'What do you think?' Josef asked.

'We can't leave her,' Bernard told him. 'If she's there we have to find her.'

Even though he was bone tired, Josef grunted his agreement. It was an unspoken code of honour amongst climbers that no injured climber should be left on the slopes if there was even the slightest chance of rescue. Besides, they had grown to like Kuni during the weeks they had climbed alongside her and they wanted to do their best for the young Japanese climber.

'How much oxygen have you got left?'

Bernard checked his gauge: 'Enough for another couple of hours.'

Josef clicked back on the radio.

'OK, this is Josef. We're going back up. But there's a limit to how long we can search, you understand?'

'Thank you so much.' The relief in Tony's voice was palpable. 'I'm sending up five of our strongest Sherpa climbers as a back-up rescue team. They're leaving camp five now with a stretcher, medical kit, food and torches. Keep us posted OK?'

'Roger and out.'

The two German climbers got to their feet and put on

their rucksacks, then, their bodies protesting with every step, they began the climb, back up towards the summit pyramid.

106

LILONGWE AIRPORT, MALAWI, EAST AFRICA

The single engined Cessna 150 taxied to the end of the runway at Lilongwe, the propellor chopping noisily through the humid African air. The pilot made his final checks, confirmed he was cleared for take off, and accelerated down the runway, the tiny aircraft bouncing as it punched through thermic air, wheeling in a tight turn and heading for Lake Malawi and the north.

The light aircraft belonged to the Red Cross, its livery white with a flying doctor's logo on the fuselage. The pilot was Richard Nyambose, a paramedic, next to him in the passenger seat a medical cool box carrying sufficient blood plasma to perform a transfusion.

Richard knew little about the nature of the emergency that had prompted his flight; all he had gathered from the call from the clinic was that a child had been injured by baboons. Richard had never heard of such a thing before—it made his blood run cold just to think of it.

Now, the Cessna was over the tin shack outer suburbs of the capital, climbing steadily at about five hundred feet a minute. When he reached five thousand feet Richard levelled the Cessna off and set his compass at thirty degrees. There was a slight headwind of ten knots or so but at least at this altitude he was confident of missing the worst of the midday convection currents.

He pulled out his navigation chart, making a quick assessment of the air miles to Chinchewe, calculating that he would be there in less than thirty minutes, then he settled back in his seat to watch Africa pass slowly beneath him.

107

NEWBURY RACECOURSE, BERKSHIRE, UK

Keiron fixed his attention on the steward in the starting box, wheeling Mazarine Town into a final nervous circuit as he tried to predict the exact moment of the off.

The other jockeys were playing the same game, each trying to get their mounts as close to the starting line as possible, anticipating the call but at the same time attempting to keep their horses from jumping the line in their excitement.

'Go on!' The wire shot up and the race was on, Mazarine Town taking an early advantage and quickly pulling clear of the melee, her immense power giving her the edge on the soft ground.

The race was a handicap chase, two miles and four furlongs in length. Mazarine Town was one of eleven runners, competing for a substantial cash prize.

Running comfortably in the front three of the pack, Keiron settled into the rhythm, perfectly in tune with his mount and appreciating—as he did every time he raced Mazarine Town—what a class act she was.

So far, so good. Five furlongs completed and Mazarine Town was holding her own. 'C'mon, Maz!' Keiron urged the horse on as they entered the first bend.

Zakira—the race favourite—was on his right, Sophie's Day on the left. Of the two horses, he rated Sophie's Day as the better rival, a tough competitor against which Keiron had raced—and lost—before.

They reached the second of the sweeping turns on the

Newbury course, Keiron noting the one mile marker as it flashed by. He held his ground, taking a waiting game as his strategy, watching for the crucial moment when he sensed the others were beginning to tire.

108

NORTH FACE OF MOUNT EVEREST, NEPAL

The crevasse walls stretched up above Kuni, frozen waterfalls of blue ice. What sky she could see—just the sliver of light revealed as a slit at the crevasse opening—was already dark and forbidding. The sun was setting on Everest and that meant temperatures would plummet to forty or fifty degrees below freezing. How she would survive such a night without a sleeping bag or shelter of a tent was something that Kuni preferred not to think about.

Kuni shuffled towards the ice wall and thrust the ice axe in as high as she could. The sharpened steel point bit into the ice, its razor edge holding firmly as she gave the wrist strap an experimental pull. Then she took the crampon set in her left hand, striking the face with the front points and achieving the same effect.

Kuni levered herself gingerly off the floor of the crevasse, kicking into the ice with her good left leg and letting her damaged right leg drag behind. She was off the ground. Maybe this could work after all, but it was going to stretch her strength and climbing skills to the absolute limit.

Kuni twisted the ice axe free and powered it into the ice once more, gaining almost a complete arm's length of height. The achievement gave her hope but she knew she could not afford to be the least bit complacent; she needed to focus as she had never focused before.

A new realization gripped her as she climbed; if she couldn't escape from the crevasse no one would ever know what fate had befallen her. The chances of any other climber stumbling into that place on the biggest mountain in the world were slim to non-existent.

Kuni could not bear the thought that her father would never know what had happened to her. She *had* to get out of that crevasse. For her father as much as for herself.

109

TERMINAL ONE, HEATHROW AIRPORT

Calder sprinted through the terminal, cursing the extraordinary length of the walkway that led to the gate for the Moscow flight. He could hear his name being mentioned on the tannoy announcements along with dire threats about his baggage being offloaded. Sure enough, when he got there the check-in staff were closing the door and the neon sign was set to 'FLIGHT CLOSED'.

'Can you let me on?' he begged them. 'I really can't miss this flight.'

The check-in staff were less than sympathetic but they radioed through to the cockpit anyway. 'I have that final no show,' the despatcher told Tina, 'I'm guessing you're already offloading his bags?'

'Not yet. We're still waiting for our slot,' came the reply from the captain. 'You can let him on.'

The check-in staff re-opened the gate and let a mightily relieved Calder take his seat. He placed his coat in the overhead bin and took his seat next to the window, grateful that he was finally on his way to Moscow after the unwelcome dramas of the stop-over.

Then he noticed who was sitting next to him: to his amazement Calder saw it was the same Japanese businessman whose bag he had saved.

'Well, that's a hell of a coincidence,' he told him. 'You going to Moscow too?'

'Yes, I'm in transit there. I've just heard that my daughter has been involved in an accident on Mount Everest. This flight is my fastest route. I can get a connection in Moscow to Kathmandu.'

110

NEWBURY RACECOURSE, BERKSHIRE, UK

As they came out of the bend, Keiron's two rivals pulled clear of Mazarine Town, snapping the jockey rapidly back to the business at hand as divots of mud and grass flew from pounding hooves.

Over to his right he could hear the roar of the crowds in the stand. He knew that Mike Sampson would be desperate for a win and he didn't want to let down the boss.

'Let's go!' he called to the horse, giving her a taste of the crop for the first time. The stinging impact goaded the horse on, and she surged forward with ten or fifteen powerful strides which put her neck and neck with the front runners.

At the one and a half mile mark a third competitor—Roman Piper—pulled past Keiron, her jockey giving her some serious stick. Still Keiron stood his ground, betting that Roman Piper's bid for glory was a flash in the pan, that she would never sustain the pace.

They galloped past the stand, the horses giving an extra burst of effort, the jockeys savouring the encouraging roar of the spectators, shrill above the drumming of hooves on heavy ground.

Roman Piper flagged, burning out quickly and giving Keiron his cue. He turned on the heat, shortened Mazarine Town's reins and gave her a few more clipped words to get her blood up.

Just under two miles, Keiron was perfectly placed,

overhauling Zakira and pulling up alongside the heavily sweating Sophie's Day.

'All right, Maz!' Keiron urged. 'Do your stuff, girl!'

111

CHINCHEWE VILLAGE, MALAWI, AFRICA

Maria Coster and her film crew had finally fixed their puncture but they got seriously lost trying to find the village of Chinchewe. There were no road signs to follow and the maze of dirt tracks which led there had tricked them into one dead end after another.

It was now mid afternoon local time as they pulled into the main square at Chinchewe and parked in the shade of a sprawling baobab tree. Within a few minutes a ragged crowd of malnourished children had gathered around the vehicle and it didn't take long to find a willing guide prepared to take Maria and her team to Bakili's house where the grandfather was the only one home.

'Good afternoon,' Maria greeted the old man, 'we are looking for Bakili. We filmed him near the lake earlier on and now we'd like to talk to him again.'

'He's guarding the fields.'

'When will he be back?' The old man shrugged. 'What about his mother, or father. Are they here?'

'No. His mother is at the clinic with Kamuzu, Bakili's brother.'

'At the clinic? Is he sick?'

'He was attacked by a baboon. They change with the famine. They fight for the crops.'

Maria turned to her cameraman. 'Now that's a hell of a story.'

'Sure is.' Renny shouldered his camera and began to film the old man.

'Is he badly injured?'

'There was a lot of blood. He was bitten here.' The old man gestured at his thigh.

'Can you tell us where the clinic is?'

The old man shook his head, confused.

'I will take you,' one of the children offered.

'OK. Jump in the jeep with us, let's go and see Bakili's brother.'

Minutes later Maria and her crew were racing down the village track, heading for the clinic.

112

COMMUTER SUBURBS OF WASHINGTON DC, USA

Shelton Marriner was not familiar with the neighbourhood he was driving through but he knew the name of the street he was looking for and he had a good map to refer to.

As soon as he located it he cruised slowly along the tree-lined residential street, checking out the numbers until he found the right house. As he had imagined, knowing what he did about the earning power of his wife's new partner, it was a substantial property with neatly manicured lawns.

There was a brand new Mitsubishi people carrier in the drive. Shelton drove a further distance down the road and turned the Chevrolet round. Then he parked up against the kerb, far enough away that he would not be recognized if his ex-wife or children happened to get curious about the parked van.

Shelton ran through the plan in his mind. He'd let them get into the people carrier, then drive up behind them into the driveway to block their exit. He wanted his ex-wife to see him, to know it was him.

Then he'd do it. He figured the blast would take out most of the house. As for his wife's new partner, Shelton had no interest in killing him. In fact he was hoping that he would leave the house before the act.

Shelton preferred him to live with the loss.

Shelton reached out and placed his fingers lightly on

the initiator switch which was mounted on the dashboard. He stroked the Bakelite toggle of the switch as he waited.

113

NEWBURY RACECOURSE, BERKSHIRE, UK

For a furlong they were virtually neck and neck, but Keiron gradually took his horse on, gaining a length and a half on his rival with three furlongs to go.

For Keiron this was what it was all about. This was what made all those dawn training runs worthwhile. Being at the front of the pack. The finish line in sight. Feeling at one with the horse.

The intoxicating adrenaline rush of *winning*.

And that was the way it was going to be, Keiron's sixth winner of the season, a pat on the back and a bonus from the boss, when Mazarine Town suddenly faltered and quickly lost her pace. She veered off the racing line, the smooth ride vanishing instantly as she limped a few clumsy steps towards the stand rails.

Then she stopped, her head hanging down.

'Maz? What's up, girl? You had it in the bag!' Keiron couldn't believe his bad luck.

The gutted jockey dismounted as his rivals thundered past, seeing immediately from the way Mazarine Town was holding her left foreleg off the ground that it was serious.

A few moments later, Mike Sampson and the vet ducked under the rails and were quickly at his side. 'It's her tendon,' the vet confirmed as he ran his hands quickly over the damaged area. 'We should have given her that scan.'

Mike Sampson swore heavily and kicked at the turf. 'She was so close to the line,' he said bitterly. 'Another few seconds and she would have had it.'

'Bloody rabbit.' Keiron spat out the words.

114

SIX LAKES THEME PARK, NEAR WINDSOR, UK

'Yes!' Dean ripped the earpiece out and clenched his fists in the air. 'Result!'

'Don't tell me it won?' Shelley put her burger down in shock.

'Ten to one! Sophie's Day! But by God it was a close run thing.' Dean planted a big kiss on his daughter's cheek and took a celebratory sip of Diet Coke, 'I knew it had to be a winner, just knew it.'

'You're not kidding us?' Sophie asked him earnestly.

'No way, princess. Your dad just backed a winner. And we're a grand richer as a result. What a nailbiter, though, it was coming second right up to the wire but the leader pulled up lame and our girl romped home.'

'How much did you put on it, for God's sake?' Shelley couldn't stop the smile across her face as she thought of the money.

'It was ten to one.'

'You didn't put a hundred pounds on a bloody horse?' Dean's wife gave him a playful punch on the arm.

'Good decision, as it happens.'

'What if it had lost?'

Dean gave her a look. 'Well, it didn't, did it? So who's the clever one now, eh?'

'We can go on holiday!' Sophie chimed in, 'or you can buy me a pony.'

Dean laughed. 'I'll definitely buy you an ice cream, sweetheart, don't worry about that.'

The family finished their burgers, Dean still ecstatically recounting a blow by blow re-run of the twelve thirty at Newbury.

'What about the roller coaster, Dad?' Sophie asked him.

'What roller coaster?'

'The Tormentor. You said I could have a go on it.'

'Well, since you've caught me in a good mood, we'll go and see.' The family left the food hall and bought some ice creams at a kiosk. Then they strolled across the park towards the big rides, Dean humming a happy tune beneath his breath at the thought of his win.

115

NORTH FACE OF MOUNT EVEREST, NEPAL

Kuni slammed the ice axe into the ice wall, a shower of needle sharp ice crystals exploding into the air and filling her eyes and nose. She was halfway up the wall of the crevasse, the strength in her arms rapidly fading under the phenomenal strain of the climb.

She ripped her good foot out of the ice step she had kicked, momentarily supporting her entire weight on her two arms, then forced it higher into the steel-hard ice, closing her mind to the sharp protestation of pain from her toes.

Suddenly she realized her breathing rate was too high. 'Breathe deep,' she admonished herself angrily, 'breathe slow.' But the frigid air of the crevasse was searingly cold and every inhalation seemed to freeze her to the core.

She had to reach the mouth of the crevasse. And this would be the one attempt. Kuni was absolutely sure she could not summon the reserves to have another go.

Kuni clenched her fist around the crampon spikes which were acting as a makeshift ice axe in her left hand. Then she swung it with all her might, just managing to get the front points to dig a few precious millimetres into the ice.

Don't look down. Kuni was only a few metres up the wall but she could not imagine the pain her shattered leg would experience if she tumbled back down onto the avalanche debris beneath her.

A few inches higher. Two and a half metres still to go. Kuni felt tears of pain and fear collecting in her eyes. Reach up. Strike hard into the ice. Don't even think about failure because failure will mean death.

116

ON BOARD FLIGHT 492 TO MOSCOW

Tina flicked the intercom switch:

'Good afternoon, ladies and gentlemen, my name is Tina Curtis and I'm your captain today on this flight to Moscow. With me here on the flight deck is first officer Graham Ravenscroft, and in the cabin you have Emma, Simon, and Tanya. Our expected flight time today is a little over three hours, and we'll be closing up the doors and securing the cabin for take off in just a moment or two. I'll be coming back to you with a weather update and more information on our expected arrival time at Moscow once we're in the cruise. Meanwhile, the cabin crew will give you the safety briefing and I would urge you, even if you are a frequent flyer, to pay very close attention. Following that, I hope you will be able to sit back and enjoy the flight.'

Her passenger briefing over, Tina and the co-pilot spent a further few minutes on completing their pre-flight paperwork then she selected 121.9 mhz and clicked to speak:

'This is skybird four-nine-two stand Tango four, requesting push back.'

'Roger skybird four-nine-two, clear push, facing west.'

Tina switched her comms to patch through to the ground engineer who was standing on the tarmac, just beneath the cockpit, his headphones plugged into the communications portal which was alongside the front wheel strut.

'Captain to Ground Engineer, how are we looking?'

'Walkway retracted and push truck locked on. Release brakes, please.'

Tina released the brakes, the roar of the push truck engine reaching the cockpit as the aircraft moved smoothly backwards.

117

SIX LAKES THEME PARK, NEAR WINDSOR, UK

The queue wasn't a long one, and soon enough Dean and his family were at the entrance to the Tormentor ride itself. That was when Dean saw the notice about the minimum height.

'You'd better stand on tippy-toes,' he told his daughter quietly, 'with a bit of luck they won't ask you to get measured.'

Sophie did her best to make herself look as tall as possible but the experienced eye of the attendant quickly picked her out of the line.

'Can I get you to stand under here, please?' the lad asked. Sophie duly stood under the measuring point, where a wooden bar stood at exactly one metre thirty centimetres, pulling a face as she realized the top of her head was just slightly shy of the height.

'That's a tough one,' the attendant commiserated, 'but you're *just* under the minimum.'

'She's not!' Dean told him. 'Look! Her hair's touching the bar.'

The attendant took a closer look. 'Sorry, but I can't let her on the ride.'

'It's her birthday!' Shelley told him.'Have a heart.'

'That's the rules. I've got into trouble twice for letting kids through when they're not supposed to and I can't do it again.'

Dean moved closer to the lad. 'We don't want to make a

fuss. But she's only about a quarter of an inch off it. Just let her on the ride will you?'

'It's not my decision, sir, it's health and safety.'

Sophie saw that others in the queue were beginning to stare at her. Her face began to crumple as tears sprang to her eyes.

'Now look what you've done!' Dean told him. 'Nice one, mate, how to ruin a little girl's birthday in one easy lesson.'

118

NORTH FACE OF MOUNT EVEREST, NEPAL

In the fading light, the two German climbers fought their way up the slope, beating against the ever rising wind. The air around them was filled with granules of ice which had been whipped off the face, their bodies hunched against the blast which threatened to blow them off their feet.

Ahead of them they could see the area that had been swept by the avalanche, a vast scar where the layers of snow had been ripped away to expose the bedrock beneath. It looked like a horrendous slide, but the two men could see that what Tony had told them was indeed true—the avalanche had dumped most of its mass into a series of crevasses they were now heading for.

'Where shall we start?' Josef shouted through the wind.

'Over there. At the foot of the ice slope.'

The face was four or five hundred metres across and right at the base was a *Bergschrund*, a vast, zig-zagging series of crevasses, some with overhanging ice and plenty of unstable snow bridges to cross.

It was complicated, dangerous ground, the type of terrain where a seemingly solid surface could suddenly give way beneath the weight of a climber to reveal a cavernous crevasse below.

Warily, the two climbers worked their way along the fault line, carefully approaching the lip of each one and peering without much hope into the depths.

'Kuni! Are you there?'

But there was no answering shout.

'We'd better rope up.' The two men tied together for safety.

119

SIX LAKES THEME PARK, NEAR WINDSOR, UK

Dean was getting nowhere. The ride attendant was holding firm to the rules. 'I can call a supervisor if you want, sir, but it's not going to change anything.'

'Leave it, Dean.' Shelley pulled him away and put her arm protectively around Sophie as they beat their way back, red-faced and fuming, into the park.

'That stupid jobsworth,' Dean raged. 'What difference does a quarter of an inch make?'

'It's all right, darling.' Shelley comforted her daughter, 'we'll come back in a couple of months and you'll get on it no problem.'

'Tell you what, sweetheart.' Dean pointed to the balloon seller standing just across the way. 'How about we buy you a couple of those special balloons you wanted earlier?'

Sophie's eyes lit up as she saw the helium filled balloons bouncing upwards against their strings, smiling as she recognized some of the cartoon characters printed on the foil.

'How much?' Dean asked the seller.

'Two fifty each.'

'Tell you what, mate,' Dean said, thinking of the thousand pounds he had just won and figuring that blowing a bit of it would be worth it to put a smile back on Sophie's face, 'how much for the lot?'

120

ON BOARD FLIGHT 492 TO MOSCOW

Tina gave her co-pilot the order to get the aircraft under power.

'Start number two.'

The co-pilot pulled the engine start switch and Tina heard the whine of the fuel pump systems as they primed the starboard jet engine. She checked her stopwatch, waiting for the muffled 'whumph' which would indicate ignition. When it came, she watched the EGT—exhaust gas temperature—gauge, to ensure the light-up was sustained correctly. She clicked off the stopwatch.

'Engine stabilized.'

'Start number one.' The portside engine fired up as the push truck disengaged. The ground engineer walked to the side of the aircraft and gave Tina an OK signal in the form of a raised arm. Tina clicked on the radio once more.

'Skybird four-nine-two, taxi.'

'Skybird four-nine-two, clear to taxi. Follow the Virgin Atlantic 747 on the parallel taxi way to two seven left. Call tower one one eight decimal five.'

Tina advanced the thrust levers, moving the aircraft forward under its own power as the co-pilot selected the new frequency.

'Tower, this is skybird four-nine-two.'

'Good afternoon, skybird four-nine-two. You're number four on runway two seven left.'

The aircraft trundled along the taxi way, Tina steering

the tiller with her left hand as the two pilots kept a close eye on other traffic.

121

CHINCHEWE AIRSTRIP, MALAWI, EAST AFRICA

Richard Nyambose reduced his air speed and turned the Cessna into the final approach to Chinchewe. The airstrip was an informal affair—little more than a strip of red dust with a tattered windsock at one end and a shed containing a couple of barrels of aviation fuel at the other.

As soon as he had landed, Martin's driver greeted him and the two of them tied the Cessna down and secured it. They transferred the cool box and other medical supplies to the jeep and took the road to the clinic, arriving to find Martin waiting for them outside.

'You're in the nick of time,' the medic told him as he took the cool box of blood product. 'Come on in. You can give me a hand with the transfusion.'

In the treatment room Martin prepared the half litre sachets of blood concentrate, snapping the first of them onto the delivery line then handing the catheter to Richard to fix to the needle.

Kamuzu's mother was watching the two medics work as she stroked Kamuzu's brow. Now, she turned to them, horror-struck as she suddenly thought of the danger her younger son could even now be in.

'My other son! Bakili! I have just thought. He is at the same field. We must go and find him before he gets hurt like Kamuzu.'

'Your other son is at the same field where the baboons attacked Kamuzu?' Martin asked. 'How old is he?'

'Six.'

Martin and Richard stared at each other in horror. 'We have to get him out of there,' Richard told Martin, 'as quickly as we can.'

122

SIX LAKES THEME PARK, NEAR WINDSOR, UK

The balloon seller thought about it for a few moments, figuring that there were about fifty balloons in total.

'You can have the lot for a hundred,' he said.

'Dean!' Shelley chided him. 'You can't afford that.'

'I just won a thousand quid, love, I can afford anything I like.' Dean gave Sophie a wink.

'Go on, Dad!' Sophie told him. 'Go for it!'

'There you are.' Dean checked in his wallet, finding that there was—just—enough cash. 'Nothing's too good for my little princess on her birthday.'

Dean handed over the cash and the balloon seller tied up the strings in a bunch and made to hand them to Sophie.

'Mind they don't take you up!' he said.

Sophie's hand made a tiny, fumbling move back as the words registered. In the split second it took her to realize it was a joke, the strings had slipped through her fingers and the balloons were going up. Dean and the balloon seller took a great leap, doing their best to retrieve the situation, but they missed the trailing strands of string by a whisker.

'I don't believe it!' Dean was gutted. Sophie's tears began again as smiling onlookers pointed up at the rapidly climbing bunch of balloons. Shelley gave Dean an exasperated look and they stood there, feeling foolish, as the red and silver mass climbed towards the clouds.

'Come on, princess,' Dean told his daughter, 'I'll get some cash out of the machine and we'll buy you some more.'

123

SAUNCY WOOD, WILTSHIRE, ENGLAND

The deer was surprisingly heavy for such a small animal, and Jamie and Will were sweating as they dragged their trophy through the thick tangles of vegetation.

Now Jamie paused, rubbing the sweat out of his eyes, and swatted a few of the flies which were buzzing around his head. Since they had been dragging the deer carcass through the woods, blowflies and blood sucking midges had been following them in a cloud.

'We're lost,' he said miserably.

'No we're not.'

'Yes we are. Else how do you explain that we're back where we shot that tree?'

Will stared at the tree, bemused, as he saw the white scar tissue where he had blasted the trunk. 'Must be another one,' he muttered, 'I know where we are.'

'Oh yeah? So which way is the road?'

Will stared around him, then spat as a fly entered his mouth.

'I know where it is,' he repeated, then set off once more into the thickest part of the surrounding forest.

'Will!' Jamie called after him. 'Just dump the deer and let's get out of here. Please!'

But Will just kept moving, tugging and wrenching the body of the deer as it snagged on roots and brambles.

'The guts are falling out of it!' Jamie observed in revulsion.

'Shut up and follow,' Will told him.

124

CHINCHEWE VILLAGE, MALAWI, EAST AFRICA

The baboons had gathered on the edge of the forest, calling fitfully to each other and barking alarm calls whenever Bakili stood up to brandish his stick.

They were clearly agitated; the young boy had never seen the creatures looking so stressed. Neither had he seen so many all at once, the size of the pack which regularly came in search of maize was normally fewer than fifteen to twenty strong. Now he had counted no less than twenty-five individuals, and there seemed to be more lurking in the shadows.

Their behaviour showed their desperation for food, darting in groups of twos and threes into the standing maize and making a grab for the unripened cobs. Time and again, as he saw each new wave of the invaders, the six-year-old child would rush into the field, wielding the wooden staff above his head and beating the ground in front of the baboons which would then scatter, screaming, into the safety of the forest.

One large male in particular was proving to be very troublesome, a ruff-necked male with huge shoulders and a muzzle covered in criss-cross scars. Bakili imagined that this was the creature which had bitten his brother.

He was obviously the ringleader—the alpha male of the pack—dishing out summary justice to lesser males who dared get too close to him with a cuff of his arm and a terrifying display of needle sharp canines. His call was deep and intimidating, a cry somewhere between a human cough and a shout of anger. Bakili kept a very careful eye on him, forcing the big creature back several times while at the same time trying to hide his fear.

125

ON BOARD FLIGHT 492 TO MOSCOW

Five minutes later, Tina and her co-pilot were approaching the threshold, moving slowly up the queue until they were next in line for take off.

'Skybird four-nine-two, after the Air Canada 757 line up and hold on two seven left.'

'Skybird four-nine-two confirm after Air Canada line up and hold.'

The two aviators watched the 757 move off on its take-off run, pausing long enough to let the turbulent back wake clear before powering the aircraft onto the runway and lining up for clearance.

Tina began the final instrumentation checks and the radio crackled into life:

'Skybird four-nine-two, you are cleared for take off. Wind two three zero at fourteen.'

There was a momentary pause as Tina and her colleague finished final checks. 'All set,' she told him.

Then the brakes were released and the thrust levers pushed forward. The aircraft moved smoothly into the take-off run, dead centre to the flight line, gaining speed with an ease and grace that always thrilled Tina even though she had experienced it a thousand times.

The aircraft accelerated down the runway, reaching take-off velocity of one hundred and sixty knots.

'Rotate.' Tina pulled back on the control column, bringing the aircraft to twelve degrees nose-up attitude, enjoying the smooth transition as the aircraft left the tarmac of Heathrow and took to the sky.

126

CHINCHEWE CLINIC, MALAWI, EAST AFRICA

Bakili's mother was pleading with the two medics. 'Let us go, we have to fetch Bakili before it is too late, come with me now.'

'She's right,' Richard said. 'We should stop those scavengers before someone gets killed, shoot them if necessary.'

'We have a gun here at the clinic,' Martin told him, 'we use it to put down rabid dogs. Do you know how to shoot?'

'No.' The pilot shook his head. 'How about you?'

'Well, yes,' Martin replied; 'but I shouldn't leave the patient.'

'Don't worry. I'll take care of him,' Richard reassured him.

Martin went to his office and unlocked the padlock to the cabinet which held the clinic gun. Moments later he returned to the treatment room, loading the weapon as he entered.

'Have you used it before?' the Malawian pilot asked him.

'Once or twice.' Martin put the gun to his shoulder, clearly comfortable with the weapon. He put two boxes of ammunition in the pockets of his jacket.

'If I were you,' Richard told him as the two men walked with Bakili's mother back out to the front of the clinic, 'I'd go for the alpha male. If you take *him* out you'll destroy the bravado of the pack.'

'I'll see what I can do.'

Richard watched as Martin joined Bakili's mother in the Isuzu. 'You take care,' Richard called after them, 'and remember, go for the alpha male.'

127

ON BOARD FLIGHT 492 TO MOSCOW

As soon as they were airborne, Tina activated the gear-up sequence, her ears tuned for the familiar whine of gears as the wheels were retracted into their bays, followed by the crisp impact of the bay doors closing correctly.

Tina watched the altimeter spin through five hundred feet.

After the stresses of the morning it felt liberating to finally be up in the air. Here, she felt in control, felt the world ran according to a set of inalienable rules. There was the reassuring thrust of the engines powering them skywards, the expert chatter of the air traffic controllers in the headphones, the always magical sight of the roads, houses and vehicles rapidly falling away beneath them.

What a dreadful morning, Tina thought as she sipped on a small bottle of mineral water. God, it felt good to be leaving it all behind.

At seven hundred feet, they hit some light turbulence as a cross-wind buffeted the aircraft. Tina checked the vertical flight director bar on the panel before her, turning the aircraft a few degrees into the wind, and making some small adjustments to the ailerons and rudder.

'Flap one green.' The co-pilot confirmed that the flaps were retracted.

'Flaps are in.'

The line to the tower buzzed. 'Skybird four-nine-two, call departure please on one two three decimal nine.'

'Thank you, tower, skybird four-nine-two confirming call departure.'

They passed over the M25 motorway, solid with traffic.

128

CHINCHEWE VILLAGE, MALAWI, EAST AFRICA

Maria Coster and her film crew were powering along the potholed track towards the clinic when the Isuzu passed them from the opposite direction.

'That was Bakili's mother!' the child they had taken as a guide told them. 'She was in the front seat of that car.'

Maria had to make a split second decision. In her mind was the thought that Bakili's injured brother might have been in the back of the Isuzu. Maybe they were moving him to a hospital. If they lost the vehicle they might lose the story.

'Turn around,' she instructed the driver, 'let's try and stop them.'

Minutes later, thanks to some hair raising manoeuvres by their driver, the film crew vehicle was pulling up behind the Isuzu, headlamps flashing to get the driver's attention. Shortly after, Martin stopped, winding down his window as Maria came to the car.

'Sorry about that,' she told him, 'we're looking for the brother of Bakili, the one who was attacked by a baboon earlier today. But I can see you don't have him in the car,'

'He is still at the clinic,' Martin told her.

Suddenly Maria spotted the weapon in the back seat. 'What's with the gun?' she asked.

'We are going up to the fields,' Martin told her, 'this woman still has a child up there.'

'Is it your son Bakili?' the reporter asked.

The woman nodded.

'We think he might be in danger from the same pack which attacked his brother,' Martin explained.

'Can we come with you and film it?'

Martin couldn't think of any reason why not.

'Sure. Just make sure you don't get in the way once the shooting starts.'

129

ON BOARD FLIGHT 492 TO MOSCOW

Tina turned to her next tasks as the co-pilot kept observation ahead, setting the air conditioning levels for cockpit and passenger cabin, then switching the nacelle anti-ice system to auto. Then she checked the navigation display, noting that the weather radar was showing no significant storm activity ahead despite the growing heat of the day.

Nevertheless, there was still quite a bit of cloud about, and as they reached their holding altitude of six thousand feet, they began passing through some quite thick cloud. The aircraft began to bounce around a little. Tina decided to wait until it cleared before she would give the signal that the cabin crew could leave their seats.

Suddenly the co-pilot pointed to Tina's wrist. 'I hope you don't mind me mentioning. You have some blood on your cuff.'

'Damn,' Tina cursed as she saw the cluster of dark red marks on her white shirt cuff. 'I hit a deer driving to work.'

'Oh my God, how horrible.'

'Yes. You could say that. The poor thing was wounded, and I went into the forest a bit to see if I could . . . if I could find it. I must have brushed against a branch or something.'

'Oh. I see.' The co-pilot's bemused tone of voice betrayed his surprise at the story.

Embarrassed, Tina took out a handkerchief and wetted it

with her saliva. Then she rubbed at the soiled patch, seeing immediately that she was only making it worse.

She rubbed harder, but couldn't clear the blood.

130

CHINCHEWE VILLAGE, MALAWI, EAST AFRICA

Bakili watched as the baboons re-grouped on the forest boundary, chattering and bickering amongst themselves. Then hunger drew them back into the field.

The child could feel tears pricking in his eyes. More than anything he wanted to abandon the field, to run back to the warmth and safety of his mother's arms. But he knew his father would be ashamed of such behaviour. Bakili had to stay.

Bakili jumped off the platform and strode into the tall crop, wishing he was tall enough to see above the maize. He gave a few whistles and screams but the animals didn't seem to be taking much notice. Suddenly, he came across the alpha male, breaking down some plants and stuffing the cobs into his mouth. Bakili charged, but to his horror the alpha male merely charged back, rushing a few steps towards his attacker, then skidding to a halt and baring his fangs with a blood curdling scream of defiance.

Bakili swung the stick above his head, round and round, holding his arms up to make himself appear bigger and more significant.

The baboon lunged towards Bakili, his clawed right arm swinging with extraordinary speed and power towards the child's stomach. Bakili brought down the staff, and gave the creature a glancing blow on the shoulder.

Then Bakili heard a noise that made his blood run cold. A rustling whisper of bodies moving through the crop, the rushing patter of scampering feet on the earth as others from the pack moved in amongst the maize behind him.

He was surrounded.

131

SIX THOUSAND FEET ABOVE SIX LAKES THEME PARK

The massive bunch of novelty balloons had been travelling upwards for exactly seventeen minutes when they were sucked into the port-side engine of Tina's aircraft.

The engine might have survived if it had just been dealing with the foil of the balloons but the situation was exacerbated by the tangle of strong Kevlar cord which bound them together—a substance similar to carbon fibre which is five time stronger than steel on an equal weight basis.

Several blades of the main fan shattered immediately, sending red-hot pieces of razor-sharp aluminium back into the secondary fan vanes which were rotating at a speed in excess of ten thousand revolutions per minute. The effect was instantaneous: the total destruction of the secondary fan vanes which—splintered and mangled—were then blasted backwards at three hundred and fifty miles an hour into the third stage of the engine—the compressor turbines. The compressor turbines then suffered a similar fate, the smaller, but even faster-spinning blades, exploding with a horrendous bang, and severing many of the fuel lines which were feeding the combustion chamber just behind.

Fuel began to spew out of the ruptured lines, much of it spilling onto the sealed combustion chamber which was glowing at a temperature of two thousand degrees. The vapour ignited, engulfing what remained of the engine, and raging immediately into the wing cavities, which had also been breached by the fast-moving metal blades.

Fuel tank number three—the largest in the wing—had also been holed by engine shrapnel and aviation spirit was now leaking at a steady rate from several fist sized holes in the underside.

132

CHINCHEWE VILLAGE, MALAWI, EAST AFRICA

The Isuzu jeep weaved its way up into the hills, Bakili's mother sitting next to the medic and pointing out the route through the maze of dirt tracks which surrounded the village. Behind them, the film crew vehicle kept as close as it could, the cameraman filming out of the windscreen.

When the track ran out, they parked up the Isuzu.

'Call for him,' she told Martin.

'What is his name?'

'Bakili.'

Martin yelled the name as hard as he could but there was no reply.

Martin shouldered the rifle and they set out on foot with Maria and her cameraman in hot pursuit. The track was steeper than Martin had expected and the medic soon found himself sweating under the tropical sun.

133

ON BOARD FLIGHT 492 TO MOSCOW

'What the hell was that?' Tina immediately looked down at the cockpit readouts, trying to make sense of the gauges, which were already indicating serious trauma in the port-side engine.

There was a muffled crump as something exploded. The aircraft gave a definite lurch to the left, and began—rapidly—to lose height as the engine noise faltered. The two pilots could hear screaming from the passenger cabin behind them.

The engine fire alarm began to sound.

'We've lost number two.' Tina watched the exhaust gas temperature gauge falling rapidly as the engine failed. Tina closed down the thrust lever to engine two and placed the fuel control switch to cut off.

'Pull fire switch,' she instructed the co-pilot. They heard the BCF fire extinguisher system rush into action but a second or two later another alarm sounded shrilly, the klaxon wailing loudly in their headphones.

'Fire in the cargo hold.'

The cockpit door burst open to reveal an ashen faced cabin director Simon Rowland:

'We hit something. The engine's on fire on the port side.'

Tina could smell the acrid scent of burning aviation spirit, mixed with the smell of combusted fabric and plastics.

134

NORTH FACE OF MOUNT EVEREST, NEPAL

'Kuni! Can you hear us?' The Germans were still calling out, hoping to hear a response which would lead them to the trapped Japanese climber. But the crevasses were deep, sometimes so deep that the two men could not see the bottom.

Halfway across the face they found themselves blocked by a huge overhanging serac, a monstrous rotten pillar of ice the size of a house which threatened the route. As they stood there, a piece big enough to crush them fell off and tumbled down the face to the glacier below.

'Let's try a bit higher up,' Bernard suggested, 'there's more crevasses up there.'

The two men began to work their way up the slope, knowing in their hearts that the search could not go on for much longer. Total dark was just twenty minutes away and the chances of finding the Japanese climber were diminishing with every passing minute.

135

ON BOARD FLIGHT 492 TO MOSCOW

Tina clicked on the radio:

'Tower, this is skybird four-nine-two declaring an emergency. We have a fire onboard and engine two is down. We're coming back round for an emergency return.'

There was another explosion from the rear of the aircraft as Tina tried to coax the aircraft into the turn.

'Dump fuel,' she told the co-pilot.

'Dumping now.'

The sound of the emergency fuel dump pumps buzzed in the cockpit.

'We're losing the flight controls.' The co-pilot was trying, and failing, to keep his voice calm. 'There's no manual control and the auto pilot's down.'

Tina felt the rudder go dead in her hands. That could mean only one thing: the control systems running from the cockpit had been severed or destroyed by fire.

'Oh my God.'

She checked the panel controls, seeing that virtually every warning light was on. A third warning bell began to ring.

'Fire in number one.'

'Release extinguisher.'

Tina watched the altimeter spinning as they began to lose altitude. The aircraft was going down.

136

CHINCHEWE VILLAGE, MALAWI, EAST AFRICA

Bakili's mother was struggling to keep up with the fast pace as they hurried up the steep track.

'Which field will your son be in?' Martin asked her.

'It is still far. The field up there near the forest.'

Martin looked higher up the hillside, trying to catch movement amongst the maize.

'Wait.' The woman cocked her head, listening intently.

'What is it?'

'I hear them.' Bakili's mother pointed up the hill. 'They are fighting. Go quickly now! Please!'

Now Martin could hear what the sharper ears of the woman had picked out: the shrill cries of baboons in one of the fields ahead.

Bakili's mother suddenly slumped to the ground in a faint. The tension, and her malnourishment, had robbed her of her final ounce of strength.

'I'll get her back to the car,' Maria told the two men. 'You two go on.'

'OK. Come on!' Martin began to run up the trail, the cameraman panting behind him.

137

ON BOARD FLIGHT 492 TO MOSCOW

Calder had been looking out of the aircraft window as the balloons were sucked into the engine. With his grandstand seat he was the only passenger to register what the silvery-red mass actually *was.*

The aircraft shook violently as the engine imploded. A sheet of flame burst from the side and started to lick along the wing. Now, Calder watched it intently, his test pilot training enabling him to take a rational overview even though he immediately feared for his life. He could see blue aviation fuel streaming from the wing tanks.

If that blows, he thought, this plane won't survive.

Panels above the passengers heads fell open to reveal oxygen masks. The robotic, eerily calm voice of the automatic message alert rang through the cabin as the attendants scrambled for fire extinguishers:

This is an emergency descent. Put the mask over your nose and mouth and adjust the headband. This is an emergency descent. Put the mask over your nose and mouth and adjust the headband.

The signal, combined with the violent swinging motion of the aircraft as the pilots fought to keep control, served to whip the passengers into an instant state of panic.

138

FIELDS ABOVE CHINCHEWE VILLAGE, MALAWI, EAST AFRICA

Bakili took a nervous look over his shoulder, seeing immediately that there were at least ten baboons scurrying amongst the maize behind him. He had to make it back to the platform. He took a couple of cautious steps back, but one of the bolder creatures rushed in and took a glancing bite at his leg, just skipping out of range as Bakili flailed with the staff.

There was blood, Bakili could feel it trickle down his calf. The sight of the blood seemed to excite the baboons even more, their cries becoming yet more frenzied as the alpha male launched another attack at the young child. Bakili parried him off, but not before he had suffered a raking blow to his chest, the alpha male's claws ripping easily through Bakili's threadbare T-shirt and inflicting a deep laceration into his flesh.

Suddenly there were five or six creatures on him, each darting in to deliver a slashing blow or a fast bite.

139

ON BOARD FLIGHT 492 TO MOSCOW

Calder turned to reassure the passenger next to him, but the Japanese businessman was already hyperventilating with terror, his fingers shaking so much he could not manage the mask.

Calder helped his fellow passenger to strap the mask on and then got out of his seat. He knew they were still too low for the oxygen masks to be strictly necessary—and although smoke was already starting to filter up through the carpeted floor of the aircraft, the visibility in the cabin was still good.

The cabin attendant spotted him:

'I'm sorry, sir, you'll have to keep to your seat.'

'I'm a pilot. I can keep your captain informed of what's happening to the wing.'

The attendant paused, unsure what to do. Then one of the port-side windows blew out near the emergency exit, shattered by the intensity of the wing fire. The attendant moved quickly away towards the rear, taking a fire extinguisher with him to fight the flames.

Calder entered the cockpit.

140

FIELDS ABOVE CHINCHEWE VILLAGE, MALAWI, EAST AFRICA

Bakili felt a sharp impact on his neck, and realized the blood was now running thick and fast.

But still he fought, whirling the weapon in an arc and aiming for the heads of his attackers, which skipped and rolled out of the way with incredible speed and agility.

Bakili knew instinctively that he had to keep on his feet at all costs, that if he fell he would be immediately savaged by the pack. So he stood his ground, striking out with the staff whenever the baboons got too close.

Then he heard shouts from some distance away.

They were faint but they were definitely voices! Calling his name. There were adults coming. His heart leapt with a surge of hope.

'Here!' he cried. 'I am here in the field! Help me! Please!'

141

ON BOARD FLIGHT 492 TO MOSCOW

In the cockpit, Tina and her co-pilot were fighting the controls as Calder entered.

'I'm a pilot,' he told them. 'Do you want me to be your eyes out back?'

Tina turned towards the American, immediately sure from his calm demeanour that he had to be telling the truth. Also what he was offering was exactly what she needed; the wings could not be seen from the cockpit and the aircraft was not fitted with observation cameras.

'What did we hit?' she asked him. 'We saw something flash past on the port-side but it happened too fast to register.'

'A mass of balloons. Sucked straight into your engine.'

Tina and her co-pilot exchanged a look. 'OK. What's the state of the wing?'

'Your port-side engine is ruptured,' Calder told her, 'I think the high pressure compressor turbine has blown. You have secondary fire in fuel tanks two and three and a range of shrapnel damage to your spoilers and ailerons.'

There was a muffled explosion from the rear of the aircraft. Cries for help could be heard punching through the rush of air from the shattered window.

142

WASHINGTON DC, USA

Shelton saw movement at the doorway of his ex-wife's house.

His eight-year-old son Kris came out with his school bag slung over his shoulder, followed by his younger brother Noel. Shelton was surprised how much they had changed in those two years, the picture in his mind had them just as they had been when he had last seen them.

Then Shelton's former wife emerged, followed by the tall, greying figure of her new partner. He was older than Shelton had imagined, in his late fifties at least.

Mr Happy Families, Shelton thought. But don't get into the car.

While the adults placed their own belongings in the back of the Mitsubishi the boys wandered on to the lawn.

A swing had been roped to an overhanging branch of a large cedar tree and as Shelton watched, Noel ran across to it and began to swing to and fro.

143

ON BOARD FLIGHT 492 TO MOSCOW

'Go and see if the fire extinguisher has put either of those wing fires out,' Tina told Calder. 'And I need to know what's left of my primary flight controls.'

Calder left the cockpit as Tina attempted to put the aircraft into a turn.

'She's not responding,' she told the co-pilot.

'Jesus. We can't turn. We're going to maintain a straight line trajectory until we hit the ground.'

'Keep heading west.'

'Like we have a choice.'

She clicked on the radio:

'This is skybird four-nine-two. Negative return to Heathrow. Maintaining westerly track.'

'Roger four-nine-two. Do you want us to alert Bristol, over?'

'Roger that, not sure we're going to make it though, we're losing five hundred feet a minute.'

144

WASHINGTON DC, USA

Shelton heard his ex-wife call to the boys and they ran back to the car and climbed into the rear. Then the two adults took their seats.

Shelton cursed. Mr Happy Families was going with them and killing him most certainly wasn't in the plan. He ran through the options in his mind, trying to work out what their morning routine would be. Would they drop the boys off at school first? Or perhaps his ex-wife would take her partner first to one of the many commuter stations which connected the suburb to downtown? He decided to follow them; he could always ram them from the rear and set the bomb off any time he liked.

The Mitsubishi reversed back down the drive and set off down the road, Shelton following a discreet distance behind.

145

ON BOARD FLIGHT 492 TO MOSCOW

The voice alarm was still going strong:

This is an emergency descent. Put the mask over your nose and mouth and adjust the headband. This is an emergency descent. Put the mask over your nose and mouth and adjust the headband.

Calder finished his observation of the wings and re-entered the cockpit.

'Fire extinguishers ineffective,' he told Tina, 'the whole wing's on fire and I'd say you have less than ten per cent movement on the port-side spoilers.'

'And the ailerons?'

'I think the control cables must have burned out. I can't see any movement at all.'

The co-pilot was giving out data as the aircraft continued to lose height: 'Altitude is three seven hundred and the speed is two six zero over the ground. We're somewhere between Reading and Swindon, forty miles out of Heathrow.'

This is an emergency descent. Put the mask over your nose and mouth and adjust the headband. This is an emergency descent. Put the mask over your nose and mouth and adjust the headband.

146

WASHINGTON DC, USA

Shelton was surprised when the Mitsubishi slowed down after just a few hundred yards. He pulled up, wondering what was going to happen, then smiled as he saw Mr Happy Families get out with his briefcase and walk up the drive of a nearby house where he was greeted at the doorway by a similarly aged male in a suit.

A colleague giving him a lift, Shelton figured with satisfaction, a car share into work.

The Mitsubishi pulled away, the boys waving out of the back of the people carrier at their stepfather.

Take a good look, Mr Happy Families, that's the last time you're going to see them.

Shelton was more relaxed now, he felt more in control of the situation. The only question now was when and where. He mulled this over as he followed the Mitsubishi into heavier traffic as they headed downtown then decided he would take them out at the school. Just as the boys were being dropped off. That really would be perfect.

147

FIELDS ABOVE CHINCHEWE VILLAGE, MALAWI, EAST AFRICA

Bakili took a few crawling movements through the maize, dragging two or three of the attacking baboons with him, their teeth locked into the flesh of his leg. Then he managed to scramble back to his feet, lashing out with his limbs at the flashing white teeth which seemed like a solid wall before him. He was focused on the staff, which since being knocked from his hands had been further scuffed and kicked deeper into the maize.

He took a step towards it, kicking out and making some headway. The staff was just within his reach, and now he picked up the weapon and turned immediately to strike wildly once more into the midst of the baboons. In between the blows he continued to scream, but his cries no longer intimidated the creatures, which merely redoubled their own screams to drown him out.

The staff fell once more from his hands. And this time he knew he would not have the strength to pick it up.

He heard the voices again, calling for him, but he could only croak feebly in reply and he knew they would struggle to find him in the thick field of maize.

148

ON BOARD FLIGHT 492 TO MOSCOW

'What's happening to the starboard wing?' Tina asked Calder. 'Why can't I roll to the right?'

'The fire's spread right through the central cargo bay,' Calder told her, 'fuel tank four has blown and your starboard primary flights are out.'

This is an emergency descent. Put the mask over your nose and mouth and adjust the headband. This is an emergency descent. Put the mask over your nose and mouth and adjust the headband.

The aircraft began to fall faster, slewing from side to side as the co-pilot fought to keep the aircraft level.

The cockpit voice alarm began to shrill a new warning:

Sink rate—Sink rate—Sink rate—

149

NORTH FACE OF MOUNT EVEREST, NEPAL

Kuni was just beneath the lip of the crevasse, trying to conserve her strength for one last big effort.

She had given her all but there was still one more metre to go. Such a short distance but it might as well have been a hundred metres for the challenge it represented.

She was breathing too hard now, panting as if she had just sprinted a half marathon, her vision tunnelled by the lack of oxygen so that all she could see now was the intimidating blue-black sliver of light still high above her.

Move! MOVE! she told herself.

She rammed the crampon spikes into the ice, forcing the needle-sharp tips into the green-blue ice wall and easing herself up with great care so that her damaged leg did not swing against the wall.

Her right arm flashed back with a determined swing. In went the ice axe.

And now came the slight overhang at the top. Could she haul herself up and over it? That would be the final test.

150

ON BOARD FLIGHT 492 TO MOSCOW

When he heard the automatic altitude alarm calling five hundred feet Calder knew he had just a few seconds to get into a seat.

The cockpit had no jump seat so he went back into the main passenger cabin. The seating area was in a state of total disarray but through the increasingly thick smoke, Calder could make out the Japanese businessman, still sitting in his front row seat with his oxygen mask on.

Next to Calder were the two rear-facing seats for cabin crew and since they clearly weren't going to make it back in time for the impact he called over to the Japanese businessman:

'Come here. Sit in one of these. You can take off your mask.'

Ren lurched over to the seats and sat gratefully as Calder buckled him into the shoulder harness.

The two men put their heads down between their knees. In the next few seconds they would survive or die.

151

CHINCHEWE VILLAGE, MALAWI, EAST AFRICA

Sweating profusely, his breathing hard and fast, Martin turned off the trail and plunged into a thicket of thorny bushes, the cameraman just a few paces behind him.

He already had a mental fix on the direction of the baboon cries and he wanted to approach the maize field under cover to give him the best chance of a clean shot. If the baboons saw the gun, he guessed, they would scatter pretty fast and the opportunity to kill the alpha male would be lost.

He glanced over his shoulder, indicating to the cameraman to keep as quiet as he could. Then he pushed on, shouldering through the vegetation, making quick progress but trying to keep the noise level down so as not to alert the baboons to his arrival.

152

ON BOARD FLIGHT 492 TO MOSCOW

'Captain, we have approximately one minute left in the air.'

The cockpit voice alarm continued its jarring alert:

Sink rate—Sink rate—too low—too low—terrain—terrain—terrain—too low.

The aircraft was coming in hard and low, way too fast for Tina to be at all confident that she could bring it down in one piece.

Where the hell were they?

Tina had lost all reference of their position—beyond knowing that their track had been broadly west from the point of the impact, she had no clear idea of where they were. There was still plenty of smoke in the cockpit and Tina had to get her streaming eyes close to the cockpit window to see anything ahead.

153

SAUNCY WOOD, WILTSHIRE, UK

Taking it in turns to drag the deer carcass, Will and Jamie were almost back to the spot where they had hidden their bikes when they heard the roar of approaching engines.

'What the hell's that?' Jamie said.

'Sounds like a jet.'

'It's bloody low enough.'

They paused, staring upwards through the trees, trying to get a fix on the direction the sound was coming from. Thanks to the dense vegetation around them, it actually seemed to be coming from all directions at once.

'Must be a military one. They're always flying over here.'

'I've never seen one.'

The sound got louder.

Then one of them screamed:

'Run! Run!'

The two boys sprinted for their lives.

154

ON BOARD FLIGHT 492 TO MOSCOW

Tina pulled her shoulder harness as tight as she could make it, noticing that they were heading for rolling, wooded countryside. At least they weren't coming down in a city, she thought. Then she looked again at the wooded meadowland they were heading for, her mind clouding with confusion as her eyes scanned the terrain.

Then she saw the Middelton folly, the ruined tower standing alone in a field.

With a shock of recognition, deep enough to chill her even though her mind was reeling with terror at the impending crash, she realized where the plane was coming down:

It was the wood—the same place where she had been delayed that very morning. Tina could see the very road where she had hit the deer.

155

FIELDS ABOVE CHINCHEWE VILLAGE, MALAWI, EAST AFRICA

Now, Bakili was beginning to feel faint, the shock of the attack and the loss of blood conspiring to weaken him. He staggered backwards, almost losing his balance again as the baboons behind him scattered.

The alpha male was stalking him, his head jerking in a series of stiff upward thrusts as he barked and called. In his eyes Bakili could see the confidence of a fighter who knows the death blow is within his reach. Suddenly, the alpha male sprang his attack, leaping up at Bakili with terrifying speed. He was going for the neck, his jaws held wide enough, it seemed to Bakili, that his entire head could disappear inside.

Bakili took the only action left to him. He turned and ran.

156

ON BOARD FLIGHT 492 TO MOSCOW

'We'll go for that strip of open land,' Tina told her co-pilot as the aircraft came in at five hundred feet.

She was looking at the same gallop that Keiron and Gary had used that morning.

'We've got to try and stay out of the trees.'

'Two twenty.'

'We're way too fast.'

The chief flight attendant's voice began to scream into the intercom: *'Brace—Brace—Brace—Brace.'*

The cockpit voice alarm switched on as they began to skim trees. *Whoop! Whoop! Pull Up! Pull Up! Whoop! Whoop! Pull up! Pull up!*

'I can't get the nose up. All hydraulic systems are gone!'

'Come back! Pull back!'

Terrain! Terrain! Pull Up! Pull Up!

Tina felt the stick shaker vibrate as it warned of the imminent stall.

The trees were rushing towards them.

Then they hit the ground.

157

FIELDS ABOVE CHINCHEWE VILLAGE, MALAWI, EAST AFRICA

Martin came to the edge of the thicket, keeping under cover as louder, more aggressive cries came from the field ahead. Suddenly, a young boy ran out of the maize towards him, behind him the entire pack of baboons. His shirt was torn, and Martin could see his limbs were bloodied and gashed. He no longer had a weapon with which to defend himself.

Behind him, moving incredibly quickly on all fours, the largest of the baboon pack was in hot pursuit. As he ran, the creature reached out and tripped the child, sending him rolling in the dust. The boy screamed in terror as lesser members of the pack rallied round their leader.

The alpha male—for Martin was sure of his identity now—delivered a tremendous blow with the back of his hand. The cuff struck the child on the head, knocking him instantly unconscious. The baboon bared his teeth, rolling his gums back and uttering a series of guttural yelps.

Martin primed the gun.

158

ON BOARD FLIGHT 492 TO MOSCOW

Calder felt the jarring first impact of trees hitting the undercarriage of the aircraft, rapidly followed by the rendering screech of tearing metal as the aluminium skin peeled back from the bottom side of the aircraft. The port-side wing dropped; the engine ripped off instantly as it dug into soft earth.

Next to him the Japanese businessman was screaming words he could not understand.

A moment later the roof became the floor as he found himself inverted, the waist strap of the belt biting painfully into his groin as 'G' forces tried to spin his body out of the seat.

He could feel the bulkhead buckling behind him as the nose of the aircraft punched through a copse of mature trees, the air inside the cabin filling with fragments of metal, seat fabric, and splintered wood.

159

FIELDS ABOVE CHINCHEWE VILLAGE, MALAWI, EAST AFRICA

Martin Curtis raised the rifle to his shoulder and swung the barrel so that he was aiming dead at the alpha male. Now he had to be fast. And he had to be sure. The young boy was lying unconscious and prone beneath the creature, his neck vulnerable and exposed. The head of the baboon was swaying from side to side in a cry of victory; the shot would have to be accurate to pick out the alpha male and avoid the boy. There was no room for error.

Then the baboon tipped his head back with a final terrible yell, his jaws opening wide to reveal deadly incisors.

Martin squeezed the trigger.

160

ON BOARD FLIGHT 492 TO MOSCOW

The aircraft gave a final lurch. All movement ended. Calder was stunned but alive. Everything was strangely calm after the horrific sounds of the impact and he now realized he could hear the groans of the wounded further into the wreckage.

Calder pulled the release mechanism on his harness and dropped heavily out of the seat.

'Help me. Help me, please.' The Japanese businessman was also still alive but clearly badly wounded with a deep gash across his scalp.

Calder unclipped the seat harness and pulled the semi-conscious businessman free.

'Head for that hole,' Calder told him.

The two men crawled over what seemed to be a cargo pallet and dropped out of the mutilated airframe onto the forest floor.

161

STUDIOS OF VIDEO REPORT INTERNATIONAL, WASHINGTON DC

Kev Grupper was watching the clock, as he always did at the end of the night at *Video Report International.* The extra material from Malawi had failed to arrive in time for him to deal with it. Bad luck, Kev thought; the story could be dealt with by the editor taking over the day shift.

Kev said his farewells to the three other staff and collected up his bag and coat.

Down in the street, he bought himself a sandwich at a corner deli and walked the short distance to the basement parking lot where his elderly Ford had spent the night.

Kev paid his five dollars to the parking attendant and drove his car up the exit ramp onto the street. Spotting a gap, he pressed on the gas, edging forward aggressively at forty miles an hour into the fast moving early morning commuter traffic. He carried on, heading for the Potomac crossing, stifling a yawn as he contemplated the forty minutes it would take him to get out to his rented accommodation in Groveton.

162

IN THE WRECKAGE OF FLIGHT 492 TO MOSCOW

Tina had taken a blow to the head in the first few seconds of the crash. Next thing she knew there was a brilliantly white light in front of her eyes, then darkness before she gradually came to.

Tina knew where she was. But it took her quite a few seconds to piece the story together. She was aware that she was hanging upside-down in her seat, suspended by her harness. There was glass in her hair, splinters of it had filled her eyes. A tree trunk had punched through one of the cockpit windows; the shattered end was pinning her against the seat back. She could hear the moan of someone in pain.

Get out of the wreckage, Tina told herself. *Before this thing catches fire.*

163

NORTH FACE OF MOUNT EVEREST, NEPAL

Kuni reached the mouth of the crevasse and pulled herself up, biting her lip as her wounded leg twisted awkwardly beneath her. Then she slumped onto safe ground, her breath coming in short, desperate gasps.

She was out of the crevasse. Now she had a fighting chance.

But first she had to rest—the ten metre climb up the almost vertical ice wall had left her completely drained and her broken thigh was now giving her constant, almost unbearable, pain. She pulled herself a short way from the mouth of the crevasse and found a relatively flat area where she could lie down. She cradled her head in the crook of one arm, the soft material of her high altitude suit comforting against the wind-scoured skin of her cheek.

You can't afford to rest.

Kuni forced herself to sit up.

If you fall unconscious now you'll never wake up.

164

IN THE WRECKAGE OF FLIGHT 492 TO MOSCOW

Tina fumbled with the waist clip, falling onto metal with a violent impact which made her gasp. Then she was fighting through a tangle of wiring, the cables of the control systems. The cockpit was filling rapidly with smoke—Tina began to cough as it entered her lungs. She was scrabbling for the doorway. Then she felt flesh.

The co-pilot.

Tina could feel a body trapped lower down in the wreckage. She tried to remember his name but found her mind a blank.

'Hello?' She reached down into the dark cavity but there was no movement from her co-pilot. She felt warmth—then a wet sensation on her hand which in that moment of confusion she thought might be spilled aviation fuel. When she pulled her hand back out there was just enough daylight filtering through the cockpit window cavity that she could see the wetness was blood.

165

WASHINGTON DC, USA

Shelton could see the school ahead, other parents dropping their children outside the gates. They were getting really close now and he was bumper to bumper with the Mitsubishi. Now he understood the journey downtown—his kids were being educated at one of the most expensive private schools in the city.

Shelton could feel his heart thudding in his ribcage, not fear exactly but more a sense of awe at his own power, at his own strength of commitment.

Now I'm going to show you, Mr Happy Families, just what kind of joker I am.

Shelton hit the brakes as a dirty brown Ford cut out right in front of him.

'Son of a bitch.' Now he was separated from the Mitsubishi. Shelton pulled out to the right to see if he could overtake the old Ford before his wife arrived at the school.

166

IN THE WRECKAGE OF FLIGHT 492 TO MOSCOW

Calder had got some air back into his lungs and now he began to notice the carnage around him: the forest resembled a war zone, with most of the trees broken off at head height.

There was a massive scar across the ground where the fuselage had dragged for hundreds of metres, scooping out tree stumps and creating a ditch which was now filled with blazing fuel. Hanging from what branches remained were the shredded remains of bodies, of ripped clothing, the fabric of suitcases, the yellow plastic of lifejackets.

A severed arm, lying next to a high heeled shoe, the nerves still twitching with life.

Calder got to his feet, trying to make some sense of the carnage. He saw that the aircraft had lost both its wings and that the fuselage itself had been split into three. Of the tail section there was no sign, all he could see was a huge area of blazing vegetation through the woods.

167

NORTH FACE OF MOUNT EVEREST, NEPAL

Kuni looked up the slope behind her, straining to see any detail in the last glimmer of daylight, trying to assess where she was. To her surprise, just a couple of hundred metres above her, she could still see the summit pole, its fluttering strings of prayer flags dancing in the rising wind.

Kuni checked her watch: it was past seven o'clock local time. Now, the Japanese climber would be alone in the dark, facing a night bivouac at eight thousand eight hundred metres with no sleeping bag, nourishment or oxygen.

She looked up the ice slope again, suddenly noticing that two dark shapes were just visible at the top end. Initially she dismissed the shapes as rocks, but the more she screwed up her eyes and looked, the more it seemed to be two climbers.

'Hey!' Kuni cried. The two climbers turned, spotting her immediately. Seconds later, they were climbing down the slope towards her.

168

IN THE WRECKAGE OF FLIGHT 492 TO MOSCOW

Calder could see that the mid section of the aircraft was lying upside down, with the seat frames punched through the roof.

Cargo pallets had spilled out of the broken end, and a consignment of some sort of plastic goods was sending a noxious spiral of evil looking smoke into the air. Bodies were everywhere, but few were showing signs of life. Many were terribly burned, the flesh blistered and blackened.

The cockpit and all of the fuselage in front of the wings had been severed from the rest of the airframe. It was lying upside down, crushed into half its previous shape, with the nose wedged between two large trees. Somehow the front section of the plane had not yet succumbed to fire but Calder could smell enough avgas in the air to know that a conflagration was a real possibility.

A scream. He heard a scream for help from the cockpit.

'Move away from the wreckage,' he told the Japanese businessman, heading for the cockpit as quickly as he could.

169

CHINCHEWE VILLAGE, MALAWI, EAST AFRICA

Martin and the cameraman raced down the track towards the valley floor, Martin carrying the unconscious body of Bakili, Renny with the camera and the rifle. They pushed as hard as they dared, risking a twisted ankle or a fall on the rocky terrain, aware that every second would count in the race to get the child to the clinic.

They reached the vehicles, the blood-soaked body of Bakili telling its own story as they fought to regain their breath. As soon as she saw the lacerated body of her second son, Bakili's mother began to wail.

'What have they done to him? What have they done?'

Martin loaded Bakili gently into the back seat of the Isuzu and helped the woman to climb in beside her son.

As soon as the vehicle had left, Renny turned to Maria.

'You're not going to believe this footage,' he told her, 'take a look at this.'

He rewound the tape and showed her the images through the viewfinder.

'Nice work, Renny, you got the whole thing. This is going to go global. We gotta get this back to Washington fast.'

170

SAUNCY WOOD, WILTSHIRE, UK

Ren had the cut across his scalp, pain across his ribs, and his arm had taken a fearful blow some time during the crash. The Japanese businessman sat with his bloodied head in his hands, breathing in toxic air and only now beginning to realize that he had just survived a major air crash.

Ren's mind flashed back to the concerns which had been with him all morning. His daughter on Everest. Was she alive?

Perhaps he could telephone base camp. But then he realized that his mobile was missing—along with his jacket. When and where he had taken it off he could not recall. Then, so faint he thought he was mistaken, he heard the sound of a mobile. Coming from the front part of the fuselage. Ren shook his head, sure that the noise would go.

But it did not. The ringing continued.

And now Ren recognized the ring tone. He stumbled, still half dazed, towards the wreckage.

171

CHINCHEWE VILLAGE, MALAWI, EAST AFRICA

Maria and her cameraman let down the tailgate of the crew 4x4 and pulled out the metallic flight cases which housed their satellite transmission equipment. Maria set up the dish, angling it with its internal compass towards the nearest geostationary satellite while Renny fired up the generator and wired up the digital betacam player so they could feed pictures and sound.

As soon as the equipment was up and running, Maria dialled the international code. Seconds later she could hear the tone ringing in the Washington office.

'Lynn, this is Maria. Tell Kev we've got more on the African story. Only this time it's pure gold.'

'Kev's gone. He finished his shift.'

'Shit. Who's the duty producer.'

'Frank. But he's not in yet.'

'Lynn. Do you know how to patch up the desk to take this feed?'

'I'm not sure . . . '

'Lynn. Get on the cellphone to Kev, get him back in there fast. Trust me, the story's worth it.'

172

SAUNCY WOOD, WILTSHIRE, UK

Ren felt wet liquid splashing on his neck as he penetrated the wreckage. His eyes started to sting. Dimly he was aware that the fluid was fuel . . .

Where was the mobile? Ren was sure it would be news of his daughter on Everest. Had she been saved? He had to tell her he was alive.

The Japanese businessman found a cavity, a coffin sized space which had been part of the cargo bay.

The jacket was there. The mobile still ringing.

Ren reached forward and grasped the jacket, reaching inside for the telephone and taking the call.

'Kuni, is it you?'

For a moment he thought he could hear the rushing of the wind. Droplets of fuel were running right into his eyes. As he shifted backwards, his body caught the frayed edges of two wires.

One spark was all it took.

173

SAUNCY WOOD, WILTSHIRE, UK

All was fire. Fire and dense smoke.

Tina found the doorway, tilted at a crazy angle almost horizontal to the floor. Her hands ran over the metal surface, searching for the handle but failing to find it. The metal of the door was red hot; Tina had burned all the skin off her palms as she had searched for the handle.

The cockpit window. Your only chance.

Tina managed to squirm her body around. Then she pulled herself over the remains of the seat and got a good look at the two cockpit windows. One was broken, but the angle at which the plane was lying meant it was digging virtually into the ground with no hope of an exit. The other was still intact, but a sturdy branch was jammed right against it.

Oh my God, I'm trapped.

Tina could feel the cockpit door begin to buckle as the flames melted their way through the thin aluminium.

174

WASHINGTON DC, USA

Kev Grupper was almost on the ramp leading to the bridge when his mobile rang. It was production co-ordinator Lynn, back in the studio.

'Kev. It's me. Can you get back in? Something's come up.'

'Come on, Lynn, you know the deal. My shift is over. Besides, what's happened to Frank, isn't he there yet?'

'Frank's just called in sick.'

'Well, he should have let you know before. I'm getting onto the freeway now and I'm in need of some sleep.'

'It's the new feed from Malawi, Kev, it's dynamite.'

Despite his fatigue, Kev's curiosity was spiked.

'What did they get?'

'Maria said it's amazing. They got this sequence where this kid is fighting a pack of baboons. It's all to do with the famine, the hunger drives them crazy. Then this guy saves the kid's life with a single shot.'

Kev was right at the ramp, if he kept on it he'd have to drive another six miles to the next exit and then the same again to get back to the studio. He made a split second decision, shot a cursory glance at his rear view and swung hard to his right to get off the ramp.

175

SAUNCY WOOD, WILTSHIRE, UK

Calder ripped back the lower branches with his bare hands, clambering up the side of the crushed cockpit until he could peer into the aircraft window. The interior was filling rapidly with smoke but he could just make out the face of the captain pressed against the glass.

'Smash the glass!' she screamed when she saw him. 'Break it!'

Calder could see flames behind her, licking under the buckled cockpit door. Even the outer shell of the aircraft was hot to the touch. What it was like inside was beyond his imagination.

'I'll get something!' he yelled to the imprisoned captain, sliding back down to the forest floor and searching quickly for something with sufficient weight for the task.

176

WASHINGTON DC, USA

The dirty white Chevrolet van ploughed at considerable speed right out of Kev's blindspot and crashed straight into the flank of the Ford. Both vehicles ground to a halt, bumpers interlocked amid crumpled metal. Steam began to pour from the front of the Ford.

'Oh no . . . ' Kev got out to survey the damage. As he did so he saw a Highway Patrol car pulling right up behind the two vehicles. He swore bitterly when he saw the cops—of all the bad luck to crash virtually in front of them. Then he saw the face of the van driver and he figured having the cops on the scene was just about the best news he'd ever heard. The van driver looked to Kev as if he was going to leap out of the van and kill him.

Psycho was not a strong enough word.

177

SAUNCY WOOD, WILTSHIRE, UK

Calder could see plenty of metal around—chunks of engine casing, jagged pieces of broken airframe and, partly buried in the soft ground, a section of hydraulic strut from the landing gear. The strut was about an arm's length, as thick as Calder's thigh, and it was heavy enough to give him a serious struggle as he wrestled it from the earth and hauled it over to the cockpit.

He manhandled the metal strut up the side of the nose section and planted his feet in a stable position on the tree trunk which had punched through the front of the aircraft.

Then he raised the strut above his head and brought it down with considerable force onto the glass.

178

WASHINGTON DC, USA

Kev watched in horror as the driver yanked open the door of the van and leapt out onto the road, the broken glass of the front headlamp crunching beneath his boots as he approached.

'Very good, boy,' Shelton screamed at Kev, 'you made that look real natural, I have to say. But you are not going to stop me.'

Kev backed up, his hands held up to protect his face as the van driver came towards him.

'Sir, I take full responsibility for . . . '

'Don't screw with me, boy, I know what your instructions were. But your little act of heroism isn't going to change a goddam thing.'

Kev flashed a look back down the ramp. He could see the two traffic cops climbing out of their patrol car not twenty metres from where he stood.

179

SAUNCY WOOD, WILTSHIRE, UK

The strut struck a glancing blow but failed to break the toughened glass. Calder raised it again, feeling the muscles in his arms quickly weakening as he lifted the eighty or ninety pound metal component once more above his head. This time he made a conscious effort to hit the middle of the window. Bang.

A fracture appeared—a star-shaped impact mark in the laminated surface of the glass.

He heard the captain scream once more:

'Harder! Hit it harder!'

The flames were racing along the edge of the cockpit now, engulfing the far side of the instrument area. Calder could see how the captain was pressing herself right against the side wall, desperately trying to keep some distance between herself and the fire.

180

NORTH FACE OF MOUNT EVEREST, NEPAL

The two German climbers were tending to Kuni, warming her with hot tea from a thermos flask and sending a radio message back to base camp to tell the world they had found her.

'The rescue team will be with you as fast as they can make it,' came the message from Tony at base camp. 'They've got everything you need.'

'Take these.' Josef gave Kuni three super strength painkillers and she gulped them down gratefully.

Far down the slopes Kuni could see a string of tiny lights as the rescue team moved towards the ridge. That was the moment she knew she would probably survive.

But seconds later a thick black cloud passed over the rising moon and Kuni had the most terrible premonition that she would never see her father again.

181

SAUNCY WOOD, WILTSHIRE, UK

Calder hauled up the strut once again, this time only managing to get it to chest height before he powered it down onto the glass.

The star-shaped fracture spread across the pane, the crazed break lines running right across now.

Calder could hear the captain but he could no longer see her—the smoke inside the cockpit was too intense. Now her screams had stopped, to be replaced by a deep, racking cough as her lungs fought the smoke.

He drove the strut into the glass once more, feeling it yield as the laminate gave way. Two more blows and he had created a fist-sized hole. Two more, and he had punched the remaining glass entirely out of the frame. Calder threw the strut aside and reached down into the cavity, his eyes streaming as smoke billowed out.

He felt two hands in the black interior.

He grabbed the wrists and pulled with all his might.

182

WASHINGTON DC, USA

Shelton had not seen the cops. He brought out a gun and waved it in Kev's face.

'Sir, I admit this was my fault.'

Kev backed away, his entire body anticipating the bullet which would surely come.

'Not good enough, you hear me?'

'Police! Drop your weapon!' The command came from the first of the two cops running now towards the scene and drawing their own weapons as they did so.

Shelton turned, starting to run back towards the cab of the van as he saw the cops. As he reached the door, he fired off a round which passed harmlessly between the two officers. He was half into the interior, reaching for the initiator switch which was mounted on the dashboard when the first of the two bullets ripped into his shoulder. The impact spun him back out of the door, onto the road, where the second bullet punched a hole right through his abdomen.

183

SAUNCY WOOD, WILTSHIRE, UK

Calder pulled Tina away from the wreckage, dragging her bodily across the forest floor and placing her in an area away from the worst of the flames. She went into a series of coughing spasms as he quickly surveyed her wounds, noting that her legs and thighs had taken the worst of the burning heat. His medical training made him instantly confident that she would survive.

Tina raised herself up on one arm and scanned the surrounding forest, her expression fearful.

'I was here,' the pilot whispered.

'What?'

'I was in these woods this morning. Looking for a deer.'

Calder looked at her quizzically. 'You're in shock,' he told her, 'you're not making any sense.'

'No.' Tina clutched at the American's hand. 'I'm telling you the truth. I was here, in this very place. This is all somehow . . . somehow meant . . .'

184

WASHINGTON DC, USA

Kev approached the dying man, watched the blood spilling from his wounds. It was a scene he had witnessed on the rushes of a hundred news reports but he felt somehow shy, ashamed almost, to be standing there as the van driver's life ebbed away.

Then his mobile rang.

'Kev. It's Maria calling from Malawi. You back in work yet, Kev? You gotta get moving, Kev, I tell you this story is *so* hot.'

185

SAUNCY WOOD, WILTSHIRE, UK

Above the background roar of fire, Calder thought he caught a cry for help. The noise came from deeper in the forest.

'There's someone alive out there,' he told Tina. 'It sounds like a child.'

'Let's go and look.' Tina was immediately alert.

'No way you're going anywhere. You lie here and wait for help with those burns.'

But the captain was already on her feet.

'This was my aircraft,' she told him, 'and I'm not so injured that I can't walk. If there's anyone still alive then I have to do my best.'

'Listen.' Calder peered into the dark interior of the forest from where the faint cry, 'Help. Somebody help,' could just be heard once again.

'You're right,' Tina whispered. 'It *is* a child.'

Calder took Tina's arm, supporting her as they picked their way barefoot through the thorny undergrowth.

Both had lost their shoes in the crash.

'Help. Somebody help us,' came the cry, more urgent now.

186

SAUNCY WOOD, WILTSHIRE, UK

The two aviators pushed their way through the bushes, which even here were festooned with a grisly array of passenger body parts and smouldering clothing. Then they saw where the voice was coming from.

Across a small clearing they could see two boys. One was standing, the other appeared to be slumped on the ground, pinned down by a piece of wreckage.

The child who was standing was holding the hoof of some type of animal but for the moment Tina did not register what it was.

'Help,' the standing child whispered, his face white with terror; 'you have to help my friend.'

Tina and Calder approached, hurrying to lift off the section of engine turbine which had knocked the boy to the ground.

'You're OK,' Tina told him, as they helped the boy to his feet. He stood there, swaying uncertainly with shock.

187

SAUNCY WOOD, WILTSHIRE, UK

The boy stared at Tina and Calder.

'It was only a deer,' the boy whispered in a trance-like voice, 'just a deer.'

'A deer?' Tina repeated.

'This one,' said the other, holding the body of the deer forward so that the adults could see it.

Tina stared. Her mind reeling. And she knew in that instant that it was the same creature that she had hit with the car that morning. The shock took all the strength from her legs and a wave of almost insane grief overwhelmed her.

She fell to her knees and pressed her face hard against the cold body of the creature.

Only then did the tears come.

188

SAUNCY WOOD, WILTSHIRE, UK

Calder and the two boys stood there, watching Tina sob urgently, uncontrollably, into the body of the deer as sunlight filtered through the trees. Rays of light punched through the smoke which had drifted over from the wreckage of the aircraft.

Then a dark but beautiful creature danced through the forest, the fluttering of its wings creating little eddies of smoke. For a few seconds the butterfly danced a halo of wingbeats around the survivors.

Calder Lawton's eyes followed it, wondering what such a fragile and sensuous creature could be doing in such a place. Then he suddenly became aware of movement in the midst of some nearby vegetation.

Calder stepped over and saw a curious thing. A rabbit had also been caught in the mayhem of the crashing aeroplane.

189

SAUNCY WOOD, WILTSHIRE, UK

The rabbit had become lost in the woods earlier that day, had wandered through the trees in a disoriented daze. Now it was fatally injured; the impact of a spinning piece of engine blade had disembowelled it, the guts spilled from the cavity of its stomach.

Calder could see tiny ribs that were jutting, shattered, from the creature's midriff and in amongst the splintered ends of bones, he could see the rabbit's heart pulsing wildly.

The butterfly flew a little lower, sensing the powerful aromas of salts and minerals.

Finally it landed, unfurling its proboscis to drink from the still-beating heart of the young doe rabbit.

As the Purple Hairstreak feasted, the creature's heart pulsed once more and then was still.

Acknowledgements

Family and friends are always in the front line when writers have a crazy idea they want to test. When it came to *Mortal Chaos* I showed no mercy, scattering early (and sometimes half-baked) drafts far and wide in the hope of feedback.

Fi, Tom, Ali, Greg and Eliza Dickinson have all been readers of early drafts and their critical feedback has played a crucial part in the shaping of the project. Chris Bradley, Nicholas Crane, Bri English, Steph Hunter and Nicola Thompson have also supported me enthusiastically from the very beginning as have Mike and Veron Thompson, Phyl and Wynne Owens and my parents Sheila and David.

Jude Holmes at Reigate Sixth Form College was kind enough to print out many copies of the manuscript for the *Mortal Chaos* focus group. My thanks to Paul Rispoli, the college principal, for allowing his students to participate.

In Spain—where I do most of my writing—I want to thank Anna, Dani and Ariadna for their love, support, and inspiration. Albert, Cristian, Jacobo, Lola, Sebastià, and Quim have also helped me with suggestions, paella, and excellent coffee.

At Oxford University Press I would like to thank Liz Cross and Kathy Webb for their editorial wisdom and passion for the *Mortal Chaos* project. These are early days but I already feel we have the makings of a great team.

Finally, my thanks to my wonderful literary agent, Alice Williams, who 'got it' from the start.

Questions and Answers with Matt Dickinson

1. What inspired you to base the storyline on chaos theory?

Chaos theory is the coolest thing in science; without it the universe would be a very boring place and so would our lives. Every time something important happens to me I get a real kick out of thinking back and wondering 'how did that *really* happen?' It's amazing how often big events in our lives are caused by tiny, seemingly irrelevant things. That sense of wonder inspired me to write *Mortal Chaos.*

2. Do you think chaos theory is true?

Chaos theory has to be true; if it wasn't we would always be able to predict what was about to happen! Physics, mathematics, economics, biology—every single aspect of our lives is affected by chaos. The tiniest change in initial circumstances leads to unpredictable results. Life would not have started without it.

3. Did you climb Mount Everest like Kuni? How did it feel?

Like Kuni, I was lucky enough to stand on the summit of Mt Everest. I was there to make a documentary and was able to film on the highest point of the world for almost forty minutes.

It was an incredible privilege to reach that place, although I have to admit I was scared stiff about getting back down again. Seventy per cent of people who get killed up there die on the descent. You can see some of my summit footage at the *Mortal Chaos* website.

Matt Dickinson on the Summit of Mt Everest

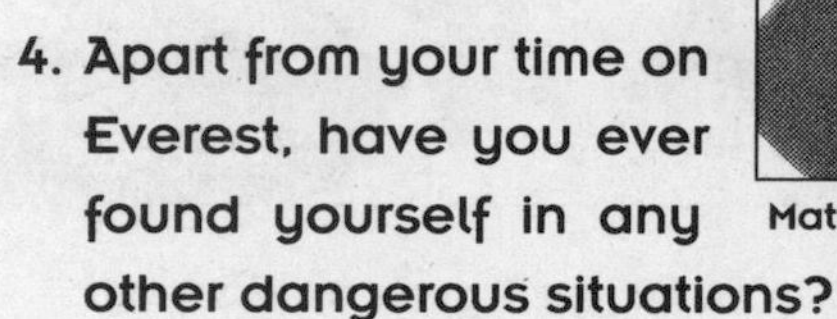

4. Apart from your time on Everest, have you ever found yourself in any other dangerous situations?

My worst moment came when filming in Antarctica. We were climbing on Mount William, on a steep ice face, when an avalanche came roaring down. For a few seconds I truly thought that we would all be killed. It was the strangest feeling, to be convinced in that moment that I would be annihilated by that awesome force. But the slope we were on was almost sheer and the avalanche shot over the top of us and crashed down on the slopes below. We were lucky that time.

5. Do you think your experiences helped you when you came to write *Mortal Chaos*?

Many of my filming experiences have found their way into *Mortal Chaos*. Situations I have seen. People I have met in the wild corners of the planet. That's one of the great things about writing: you can file incidents and events away in your mind with the plan to use them in a book at a later time. So there's a lot of 'real life' actuality in *Mortal Chaos*!

6. There's so much going on in *Mortal Chaos*. Did you have some kind of plan before you started writing so that you could see how all the different stories would weave together?

I made an intricate plan to work out the plot of *Mortal Chaos.* In fact at one point virtually all the walls of my office were plastered with Post-it notes! I love working out the connections and there's always that 'eureka' moment when you find a weird or wonderful link between the characters. The action is based on cause and effect so I have to have a clear idea what's going on from the beginning. One missing link and the whole thing can collapse!

7. There are lots of amazing characters in the book and they really come to life. Do you have a particular favourite? Or a character who is similar to you?

My favourite character is Bakili. I did some filming in Malawi once and we met young lads just like him who stay out all night in the fields to chase away predators and scavengers. He is a courageous character who is loyal to his family and he doesn't back down from guarding the maize even though he is terrified of the baboons. When it comes to the most similar character I would have to say Kuni—she loves to climb and so do I.

8. You've written a second *Mortal Chaos* book. Did you find writing it easier or harder than the first one?

I loved every minute of writing the first *Mortal Chaos* and, if anything, the second one was even more fun. The reason was that I felt more confident in the concept and had a stronger feel for what the reader would enjoy. So there's a bit more renegade action in there and a few even weirder connections than the first. And the third: well, watch this space!

Trekking in the Alps

9. Do you have any tips for readers who would like to be writers?

Yep. I'd say write about the things that you are into, the stuff that excites you. Look to your own world, the things that interest you or make you angry, and you will find strong things to make a theme for a short story or a book. Writing a long book or a novel is intimidating so it helps to think of it as a series of short stories. Above all don't think that it has to be perfect; most of the successful writers I know have the following tactic: get the first draft done as quickly as you can. Then re-write and re-work it until it is how you want it to be. Get feedback from friends and family.

The chaos never ends . . .

Are you ready to be blown into

DEEP OBLIVION

1

21ST FLOOR, UNFINISHED OFFICE BLOCK, SYDNEY, AUSTRALIA

The butterfly was an Australian Painted Lady, a lost survivor of a migrating tribe. She was exhausted and beaten up, living out the last chapter of an eventful and frighteningly short life. Her wings spoke of a thousand miles of hard travel, their edges frayed and ragged.

Some months earlier, in the first ecstatic flights of her young life, this creature had danced among the Foxtail Palms and thousand-year-old Kauri trees of the forests of Queensland, tasted the nectar of Illawarra Flame flowers and feasted on candy-coloured orchids as big as your fist.

Now she was stressed and alone, trapped on the twenty-first floor of an unfinished office block high above Sydney, a dusty deathtrap devoid of liquid or plants.

It was just past 7 a.m. on the 31st of December. The last day of the year. The Australian Painted Lady shrugged mortar dust from her tattered wings and beat herself against the glass in her quest for freedom and light.

2

CENTRAL BUSINESS DISTRICT, SYDNEY, AUSTRALIA

The security guard was a twenty-four-year-old guy by the name of Markos Dean. 'Marko' to his friends.

Today he had the morning shift. From 6 a.m. until 2 p.m. this part-constructed shell of a building was Marko's domain and, right now, he was on his hourly patrol.

He reached the twenty-first floor where a fluttering movement caught his eye. He walked over to take a look and, as he got closer, he realized it was a ragged-looking butterfly, beating itself crazy against a window.

If there was one thing that Marko hated more than anything else it was butterflies and moths. Something about their fat, hairy bodies just made him squirm.

He put on one of his leather gloves. He slammed his palm hard against the glass in an attempt to kill the butterfly. But the creature was fast, and he missed it by a couple of inches.

Instead, the impact had the most surprising effect: the glass panel popped right out of its frame and fell away from the building. Marko leant forward in shock, watching in horror as the huge pane of glass fell towards the street below.

3

OPEN OCEAN, NEAR SYDNEY, AUSTRALIA

The cruise ship was the MS *Cayman Glory*, weighing in at 45,000 tons and cruising now towards Sydney harbour at eighteen knots. She was one of a new generation of super-deluxe vessels, fitted out to the exacting standards of a five-star hotel and catering for an international clientele who like their luxury and are not afraid to pay for it.

The Captain was Stian Olberg, a stout, fifty-six-year-old Norwegian who was celebrating his twenty-fifth year at sea.

'Reduce speed. Eight knots,' Olberg told his first officer. He nodded to the radio officer, 'Raise Harbour Control.'

The radio officer switched his VHF transmitter to Channel 13. 'Harbour Control. This is MS *Cayman Glory* reporting five miles south-east of pilot boarding ground. ETA twenty minutes.'

Captain Olberg felt the deck beneath his feet tremor slightly as the MS *Cayman Glory* reduced speed. He took a sip of black coffee and put on his sunglasses.

It was a fine day for cruising.

4

CENTRAL BUSINESS DISTRICT, SYDNEY, AUSTRALIA

Hannah had been awake all night and she was feeling sick as a dog. But the world around her was waking up, and that might mean a few coins to help her through the day.

Hannah had been living rough in Sydney's parks for a good few weeks, long enough for her to have learned that it was a dangerous place for a seventeen-year-old girl to be. At night she got hassled by drunks. During the day she was endlessly moved on by the police.

She was horribly aware that she looked a mess: the dreadlocks she had once been so proud of were matted and filthy. She couldn't go home: the very thought of returning to her drunken bully of a father was too much to contemplate. Her mother was long gone and had cut all contact years before.

Now, Hannah sat on the pavement outside the shiny new building and brought out her tin. Almost immediately a good Samaritan threw a couple of coins into the pot. 'Thanks, mate,' she called after him.

An instant later she saw something flash through the air.

5

CENTRAL BUSINESS DISTRICT, SYDNEY, AUSTRALIA

The pane of glass hit the roof of a passing truck in the street below. The impact speed was about one hundred and forty kilometres an hour. Twisting as it fell, it was precisely flat relative to the ground as it cannoned into one of the reinforced steel frame supports that held the canvas truck roof in shape.

The effect was a veritable explosion of glass as the huge laminated pane ripped itself into thousands of razor-sharp shards.

Hannah the beggar was one of the closest to the impact. She was covered in glass but, miraculously given the size of the pane, didn't seem to have been hurt. At least not yet.

Others were not so fortunate; a smartly-dressed businesswoman was reeling with a vicious cut to the forehead. The rider of a motorbike ripped off his helmet and approached her, pulling out a tissue to press against her wound.

Hannah heard him reassuring the woman: 'It's OK. I'm a doctor.' She also noticed that the man had left the engine of his motorbike running.

6

CENTRAL BUSINESS DISTRICT, SYDNEY, AUSTRALIA

Hannah's eyes were glued to that motorbike. A ten thousand dollar Honda Transalp—just waiting to be ridden off. A gift. Hannah had been taught how to ride by her brother and could handle even the biggest dirt bikes on rough terrain.

Hannah watched the scene closely for a few more moments. Amongst the chaos she could see the owner of the bike; he was helping out an elderly couple who had suffered some superficial cuts from the mysterious flying glass.

Hannah leapt onto the Transalp and kicked it into gear. She gave it plenty on the throttle and raced at breakneck speed down the street. The owner of the bike shouted out—a cry of shock—as he realized his bike was being driven off. But Hannah swerved around him and made it out of the melee.

She felt the wind rip through her hair as the bike accelerated with a satisfying surge of power. It was, she decided as the adrenaline of the moment kicked in, a lot more fun than sitting on a pavement waiting for coins.